Sick to death of being run after for her money, Thea ran away herself—to Drumlarig in the Scottish Highlands, where she had been happy when she was a child. But she only ran into more trouble, when she took a job as housekeeper to Logan Murray, without telling him who she really was. And with Logan, a new set of problems developed . . .

DECEPTION

BY

MARGARET PARGETER

MILLS & BOON LIMITED
15–16 BROOK'S MEWS
LONDON W1A 1DR

First published 1980
Australian copyright 1980
Philippine copyright 1980
This edition 1980

© Margaret Pargeter 1980

ISBN 0 263 73393 9

Set in Linotype Plantin 10 on 11 pt.

*Made and printed in Great Britain by
Richard Clay (The Chaucer Press), Ltd., Bungay, Suffolk*

CHAPTER ONE

THEA ANDREWS paused by the weatherbeaten bed and breakfast sign and stared up at it, trying to read it properly in the fading light of the December afternoon. It wasn't so much this information, which looked as though it had been there for countless ages, which held her attention, but what was printed below it on another rough piece of boarding.

Housekeeper required, it read. No wages but good home to right person.

Wryly, Thea shrugged. It could be of more interest to dogs or cats! Surely someone was being over-optimistic? Not that it was any of her business. A bed for a few nights, until she decided what to do, was all she required. She tried to take no notice of the strange notion which gripped her as she continued to study it, that it might be of more use to her in her present predicament than the advertisement above it.

Housekeeper wanted? Getting wetter by the minute, Thea stood there frowning, lost in thought. Could a girl of her age, not twenty-one until her next birthday, qualify for a post like that? They were bound to want someone older and experienced, and she was neither. She did know something about running a house and she was sure she wouldn't be frightened of hard work, but she knew nothing of life up here in the Western Highlands.

Sighing uncertainly, she eased the rucksack on her back so the straps cut less deeply into her slender shoulders. The night was wild, the wind blew strongly and the rain came down as though the clouds had been saving up for months. The old, shapeless anorak she wore didn't keep out the wet, and the tight jeans, which she had reached

5

for yesterday in such a hurry, might have been glued to her long, slim legs.

Impatiently she pushed back the strands of wet hair which a gust of wind kept blowing over her eyes. As paying guest or domestic help, what did it matter? It was far more important that she found shelter for the night. She hoped she wasn't foolish enough to imagine she could get soaked and lost in this part of Scotland and get away with it. Near the bed and breakfast sign was another, with the name Drumlarig painted on it and an arrow pointing down a narrow road. This must be the place she had set out to find, the Highland estate where she had been born and lived until she was five. Hadn't her mother said that if she was ever in need of help, the Murrays of Drumlarig would never turn her away?

But as Thea began walking in the direction the arrow pointed, she had to tighten her cold lips to stop them from trembling. Ashamed of such weakness, she tried to pull herself together. Self-pity, she realised wearily, wouldn't help her now. Unlike her mother, she should never have found it necessary to be seeking help from anyone. If she had kept her head and been sensible enough to take heed of the several incidents which ought to have given adequate warning, she might still have been in her comfortable London flat instead of trudging along a desolate country road in the dark.

It seemed incredible that she hadn't believed the world was full of those ready to take advantage of a lone girl who had been left money. If she had anything left to be thankful for it was that she had had her eyes opened before any real damage had been done. After a little of the bitterness had subsided, she might have reason to be grateful to Jerry Banks, and his so-called sister.

If Jerry was the last in a succession of friends with hard-up stories, he must surely have been the worst. Hadn't he persuaded her cleverly that she must have a holiday in

Switzerland, making it seem like a favour that Pam and he should be willing to accompany her? St Moritz for Christmas—Jerry had suggested it would be great fun. He hadn't added, with Thea paying, of course. What an idiot she had been! How easily he must have gained the impression that she was as eager to part with her last penny as he was to spend it. All the money she had inherited but not been able to lay hands on until her grandmother had died.

The greater part if this money was still tied up until she was twenty-five, but she wanted none of it now; it had brought her no happiness. On returning from Switzerland she had consulted the family solicitor about giving the whole lot of it to charity. In coming here, Thea had brought very little with her. Only a few pounds to keep her going and pay for her keep.

Her feet stumbled as her thoughts went back to St Moritz. They had booked in at one of the smartest hotels, full of minor titles and top international pop stars. Mink and ocelot coats had mixed freely with feather-lined ones and hand-knitted ones. Thea had found it all rather frightening at first, but Jerry had a caustic wit, and in a very short time he had had both girls giggling.

Again, Thea stumbled, not feeling over proud of herself as she remembered her amusement at Jerry's low-toned but unkind remarks. But this wasn't as painful to recall as her rude awakening outside Pam's bedroom door.

She had discovered a piece of Pam's luggage, mistakenly mixed up with her own, and decided to take it to Pam herself. Because of some mysterious change in the booking arrangements, Jerry and Pam were on the floor above.

Thea wasn't sure what had made her pause outside Pam's door. Perhaps she hadn't been certain she had got the right number. The door had been slightly open and she had heard Pam speaking. Smiling with relief, she had been about to knock and walk in when she had heard Jerry's voice.

'Pam, my sweet! I promise it won't go on much longer. Anyway, sooner or later the little fool's going to start getting suspicious. I know you don't like it, but just keep thinking of all the wonderful lolly she's spending.'

'I'll try,' from Pam.

'That's more like it!'

There had followed a peculiar silence, then to Thea, transfixed to the spot, Jerry's voice seemed to purr.

'I almost have her promise of a lump sum, my darling. Not a fortune, but enough to keep us in la crème suprème for a good few weeks. Who knows, if I'm lucky with the dice we could turn it into twice as many.'

'But she thinks I'm your sister, and that you want this money to bolster up the family business.' Thea, though completely stunned by shock, sensed that Pam wasn't wholly convinced. 'Why not marry her, Jerry, instead of me? I think she's beginning to expect it.'

Jerry had laughed then, unforgivably. 'If it wasn't that she doesn't come into real money until she's twenty-five, I just might have. But,' his voice dropped so softly Thea had to strain her ears to hear, 'if I ever marry anyone, Pam, it will be you. We definitely have something going.'

'Maybe you have with Thea too? She wouldn't be the first!'

His hoot of sarcasm had been an insult. 'Don't be daft, my sweet—she's still wet behind the ears. The odd kiss is all I'm allowed, although I confess, out of sheer curiosity, I have tried to go a bit further. She's certainly got a pretty enough face and you couldn't fault her figure, if she doesn't know yet what it's made for.'

'So—in the meantime,' Pam had sounded cool but harshly resigned, 'you continue leading a double life? Her by day and me by night.'

'You're quite poetic, darling! Yes, to both. And if you want your bills paid you'd better settle for it, too. Just be thankful I found another little sucker to dupe.'

'Surely you think I'm worth it?'

'Come here, my sweet, and let me show you!' Jerry's laughter, low and silky, had faded into another of the silences which no longer needed explaining.

Everything for Thea had been hazy after that. Even now she couldn't remember each detail of her immediate movements, stunned shock not being the best material on which to record them. Instinct, she believed, must have governed her reactions more than anything else. She had simply turned around and come home, never quite sure how she had managed it. Before leaving the hotel she had left Jerry and his so-called sister enough cash to see them through the next two weeks, realising it might be cheap at twice the price to avoid the risk of them following her. Not for a moment did she doubt that they would stay at the hotel, greedily extracting the last bit of anything they could get.

After the first shock had worn off, such self-contempt had begun eating at her soul that it had scarcely been bearable. Amazement at her own gullibility and blindness had seared her with endless despair. Her delicate young face, too sensitive and vulnerable for her own good, was often streaked with tears. Like a curtain the scales had fallen from her eyes, but, unlike a curtain, the pain couldn't be picked up and neatly folded away. It had hurt, and gone on hurting. It was then she had realised it might take something drastic to remove it.

She had known she must leave London. Not just because Jerry and Pam might try to seek her out again, but for her own good, to give her time to sort herself out. Most of all she wanted to escape from the money which seemed to have brought her little happiness, which might easily have brought about her complete downfall if she hadn't discovered Jerry's duplicity in time. With this in mind she had gone to her solicitor, but he had begged her not to do anything too hastily. If she still felt the same in six months, however, he had promised to see what he could do.

It was while she was thinking despondently of this that she decided impulsively to go to Drumlarig. Her mother's advice had kept coming back: 'When you grow up, Thea, if you ever need a refuge go there. They took me in before you were born, when I had nowhere to go. They would never turn you away.'

What had really driven her here? Thea wondered. Her present unhappiness, or an unconscious desire to find the missing pieces of a jigsaw which for her had never been complete? Something or someone, outside common sense, must have guided her footsteps to this godforsaken part of the country. Yet, as she trudged along the lonely, potholed road, she discovered an odd sense of homecoming.

Although she tried to concentrate on the potholes, her mind wandered. The Murrays, if they were still here, would never connect her with the thin, ragged little waif, whose thick head of fair hair had made her seem incongrously top-heavy. It had been different after they had returned to England, where it had been cut and properly shaped until it was much as it was now, silky fair and beautiful.

She couldn't have known how she had looked then if it hadn't been for the snapshot. A quick snap someone had taken of Thea with Logan Murray, the middle one of the three Murray brothers. Thea could barely recall any of them, but she seemed to remember her mother saying that the eldest one, James, hadn't been well liked. They had left Drumlarig when her mother discovered she had an extremely weak heart and might easily die. And if she didn't take Thea to her grandparents she could rob her of her rightful inheritance.

The road dipped and suddenly Thea was up to her waist in a fast-flowing stream. The current, though swirling, wasn't strong, so fortunately she was able to wade through it. The light was fading so rapidly it was getting difficult to see where the water was deeper in some places than in others. It lay on the road in pools and the sound of it rushing down the hillsides came to her even through the darkness. It was wild country, full of heather and hills and loneliness. Curiously she wondered why such isolation should fill her with a kind of excitement, rather than terror. Was it just that she was too wet to feel frightened?

At last she came to a house—not a very welcoming one, by the look of it. It was too big, too gaunt, and, with only one small window lighted, it reminded her of a sleeping giant opening one eye at the sight of an approaching victim. A glimmer of whiteness behind it could have been water or merely a trick of the fast-fading light. Whatever it was it was soon swallowed up in the encroaching darkness.

She knocked on the door, her fingers so frozen she found it difficult to lift the heavy knocker and not caring for the way in which the sound of it echoed inside. Even from here she could hear it booming eerily. It was a lonely, hollow sound, as if the house was empty. Panic-stricken for a moment, Thea tried to consider what she would do if it was.

Relief poured through her, bringing a little warmth back to her veins when the door opened. She saw two bright dark eyes and heard a young voice bidding her good evening.

'Did you want something?' the owner of the voice, a small boy, asked, without inviting her in.

'Yes,' she replied, through chattering teeth, deciding not to stand on ceremony. She was startled to find so young a boy here—he couldn't be more than seven or eight, but he was obviously very self-contained.

'Have you come about the job?' he enquired suddenly, before she could go on.

'What job?' she repeated after him, numbly.

'We're trying to find a housekeeper.'

'Oh, I see.' She had forgotten about that. 'Well, not really ...' He sounded so anxious she found a straight denial impossible. 'I did see your advertisement, though, at the end of the road, under the bed and breakfast sign.'

'Oh, that?' He shrugged thin shoulders. 'No one bothers with that any more.'

Dismay made Thea stiffen. 'Then wouldn't it be kinder to take it down? It's very misleading.'

'We've been going to.'

'I see.' A shower of rain from behind her blew straight into the boy's face. She noticed he didn't so much as flinch. It was almost as if he had been taught to endure whatever life chose to throw at him. Strangely disturbed, Thea frowned. His parents were probably too strict—a thought which prompted another. It might be easier to speak to his parents as soon as possible. 'Are your father and mother in?' she asked, trying to be diplomatic.

His small hesitation was barely noticeable. 'My father is.'

'Do you think I could speak to him, then?' Casting a hasty glance over her shoulder at the wild bleakness of the glen, she added quickly, 'Even if you've stopped taking in paying guests, I think I'll have to ask if you could put me up, as I don't think I'd be able to find my way back to Fort William tonight.'

'Then you'd better come in.' With an uncertain flicker of heavy lashes, the boy stood aside, but Thea could see he was wary. The hall was cavernous and dark. Shivering afresh, she felt no warmer here than she'd done outside.

The boy didn't move. When she glanced at him enquiringly, he said slowly, 'I'm not sure if I'm doing the right thing. You won't be able to see my father, you see. He's ill in bed.'

'Ill?' Disconcerted, she stared at him. 'But if your daddy's in bed, who's looking after you?'

'I don't need anyone.'

'There must be—someone?'

He sighed, patently tired of her questions. 'There's only old Martha, but she can't look after herself. She'll have to go soon, Father says, if we can't find a housekeeper.'

Small wonder they hadn't! Cold and hungry as she was, the scornful thought flashed through Thea's head. No wages and a house this size to look after, not to mention a young boy and old lady. His father must believe in miracles —if he hadn't found one yet!

'What's your name?' he forestalled her almost similar query.

'Oh, I'm Thea Andrews,' hastily she introduced herself. 'Are you a Murray?'

'Yes,' his well-shaped dark head tilted proudly, 'I'm Jamie, after my grandfather.'

He must be the son of one of the brothers. Hesitantly she said, 'I don't want to disturb your father if he's ill, but I'm sure he wouldn't mind, Jamie, if you showed me where I could change out of my wet clothes. I have dry ones in my rucksack.'

This he was eyeing with some interest, but all he said was, 'I can take you upstairs if you like.'

As if deciding suddenly to trust her, he led the way across the huge hall, up the wide staircase. Simultaneously they halted outside a bathroom door. 'I'll wait downstairs, in the kitchen,' he informed her, turning away.

With a perception which surprised her, Thea knew he was frightened. 'Is your father very ill?' she asked gently.

As Jamie threw her a glance, very dark and anxious, Thea knew she was right. 'He's quite ill,' he nodded.

'Hasn't the doctor been?'

'No.'

She controlled her impatience with difficulty. 'For goodness' sake, why not?'

He looked as if he considered she should have known. 'The lines are down and the burn is up.'

'So you've no telephone?'

'No. We won't have until the men come to mend the wires.'

'Then who's looking after your father? Martha?'

'No,' his voice hardened scornfully, 'she's gone to bed because she's old. I'm taking care of him.'

'You?' Thea was unable to hide her startled reactions. It seemed incredible that a boy of his age should be anywhere near a sickroom, let alone trying to manage it!

She regretted her brief exclamation when his face fell; she had not expected him to look so chastened.

'I've done my best,' he mumbled unhappily, 'but I suppose I haven't been able to do much. I made some soup, but it's a bit of a mess. Martha tried some before she went to bed and said it was only fit for pigs.'

Thea frowned, deciding not to give Martha full marks for tact. This boy might try to act like an adult, but no one could mistake him for anything but the child he was. 'Look,' she offered impulsively, suddenly not able to bear such hidden pathos any longer, 'if you wait until I change, I'll see what I can do for your father. Unless, of course, you mother will be home by then?'

'No,' his green eyes were very steady, 'she won't be coming home.'

The way he said it almost made Thea shiver as, without adding anything more, he turned again to make his way downstairs.

To her surprise, because the house seemed so old and neglected, the water was hot. Quickly she stripped off her wet clothing to take an equally quick bath. She feared she might be taking advantage of hospitality that hadn't yet been offered, but she wouldn't be able to help anyone if she got pneumonia. The clothes in her rucksack, owing she guessed to her immersion in the burn, were unfortunately all as wet as those she had just taken off. There seemed nothing for it but to borrow the towelling robe which hung behind the door. It must belong to a man, as the shoulder seams came nearly down to her elbows, and the width of it might easily have gone round her twice. What did it matter? Indifferently she attacked her damp hair with a warm towel. She was lucky to have found anything in this sparsely appointed house!

As she ran downstairs again, it struck her as strange that, while she could remember nothing, she had known instinctively where to find the bathroom, just as she found her way, unerringly to the kitchen, as though in her mind she followed the trotting ghost of a five-year-old child.

In the kitchen she found Jamie by a large wood-burning stove, curled up half asleep in an old armchair. Compassion caught at Thea's heart, as she stood for a moment watching him. In sleep, without the dignity he assumed when awake, he looked oddly pathetic, and hard on the heels of pity she felt the first stirrings of anger against his father, who was probably suffering from nothing worse than a heavy cold. After the soaking she had had, she might be more in need of care and attention than he was. As if to emphasise this she sneezed, and Jamie's green eyes flew open.

Immediately his small face brightened, as he found the sight of her reassuring. Thea concluded, and rightly, that with her hair dried and combed, she appeared more human than she had done a little while ago.

She smiled, which had its effect, had she but known it, on even so young a man. Involuntarily he smiled back before, obviously thinking he had unbent too far, his boyish eagerness was replaced by a scowl.

Quickly, to divert him, she spoke lightly. 'Hello, Jamie, I'm back, but I've not managed as well as I thought I would. I'm afraid I've had to borrow this robe. The clothes I took off are still wet and so are those in my rucksack.'

'That's all right,' he replied carelessly. 'It belongs to my father.'

'I thought it might.' She hurried on, as this information, though not unexpected, disturbed her, 'I wondered if it would be a good idea to go and see your father now?' She wasn't quite sure whether it would be or not as, apart from Grandfather Andrews, she had scarcely ever seen a man in bed, and certainly not a stranger. Yet, if Mr Murray was very ill, mightn't it be on her conscience for ever if he passed away before morning and she had done nothing to help?

To her utter astonishment, Jamie was alarmed. 'You can't go and see him,' he exclaimed. 'He'd be absolutely furious if I let you.'

'But—if he's sick?'

'It wouldn't matter, he'd find out. He always does.'

Staring at Jamie's pale, stubborn face, she racked her brains fiercely. Her dislike of Jamie's father was growing, but she tried to be sensible. She must think of poor Jamie.

'I've had some nursing experience,' she said rashly.

'Oh . . .' Jamie's eyes widened as he slowly digested this information. 'So you're one of those, a nurse! Why didn't you say so?'

'Well,' deciding to skip any slight discrepancies, 'I've hardly had a chance, have I?'

Alarm feathered in her breast as he shook his head but became almost tearfully excited. 'You'll be able to make him better, Miss Andrews? I'm so pleased I let you in. Father will be, too, won't he? I mean, when he wakes up and finds you're a nurse.'

'I—I should think so,' she swallowed an accumulation of guilt in her throat. 'And please call me Thea.'

'I will,' he agreed, so absently she knew he wasn't with her.

Thea's face softened. The recipient of such devotion might not deserve it, but it was very touching to see. 'After I visit your father, I'll make you some supper and then take you to bed.'

'I can take myself to bed, thank you.' The dignity was back with a vengeance, as he proudly lifted his small chin. 'Now,' he said manfully, 'if you'll just come with me.'

About to follow, Thea suddenly hesitated. 'Don't you

think we should take him some tea or something? Or might it be better to ask what he wants first?'

'He's unconscious.'

'Unconscious!' Without meaning to, she exclaimed in alarm. 'Why didn't you tell me before?'

'You didn't ask.'

She was astounded, truly shocked against Jamie's stolid acceptance. 'Now what shall we do?'

'But you're a nurse!'

A nurse! If only she had been. She suspected it wasn't the last time she was to regret claiming to be any such thing! Wholly harassed, she paused. She could confess, yet if it brought comfort to this neglected little boy mightn't a little twisting of the truth be justified?

Quickly she pulled herself together, dismissing the last qualms of guilt. Tiredness was sweeping her in such waves and she knew if she didn't make an immediate effort she might soon be beyond it. 'Lead the way, Jamie,' she managed a calmness of voice which she could see made him feel happier. 'I was startled, that was all. Of course I'll be able to cope.'

For the second time they went up the stairs together, their shadows following them darkly along the high old walls. This time they went quite a distance along the corridors, until they came to the very last door. The whole house was icy and badly lighted. Even before they reached Mr Murray's room, Thea was cold again.

Inside his bedroom the lighting was just as dim. For a moment she could only see the shadows which had been pursuing them since they left the kitchen. Like the rest of the house, this room was big, the furniture of the same dimensions. Apprehensively her weary eyes fell on the bed and barely in time she suppressed a startled gasp. With a fastidious little tremor she drew back as her heart seemed to leap somewhere in the region of her throat. It mightn't be sensible, but there was something so aggressively masculine about the man who lay on the bed that she felt almost frightened.

The room, like the passage outside, was freezing. She was sure he should have been under the blankets, but these lay in a tumbled heap at his feet, where he had obviously thrown them. He lay on his face, his arms hugging his pillows, bare from the waist up. A little below that as well, Thea saw, where his pyjama trousers had slipped. Her eyes, clear and innocent, darkened with a kind of bewildered fascination as her glance travelled the length of his six-foot-plus frame. She felt peculiar, out of her depth, yet conscious of a terrible prickling awareness.

Drawing a sharp little breath, fraught with increasing apprehension, she allowed her gaze to return to the powerful shoulders, to waver on the strong column of his neck before continuing up the back of his dark head. His hair, like Jamie's, was thick and springy, his illness—whatever it was he was suffering from—not yet having had time to drain the vitality from it. She couldn't see his face, which was still buried in the pillows, but all of a sudden, she wasn't sure she wanted to. What she could see seemed to be more than enough!

'This is my father.' She became aware of Jamie's tugging at her sleeve impatiently while shooting uncertain glances at her confused face. It was quite clear that, as he believed her to be a nurse, he expected some immediate action!

'Yes.' Forcing herself forward, she hoped her reluctance didn't show. His father was just a man, after all, not a wild animal to be afraid of. Jamie seemed quite certain he was unconscious, but she felt she must make sure. From the bottom of the bed, she said, 'Good evening, Mr Murray.' Somehow that sounded incredibly foolish!

Jamie was proved right, as there was no reply, only the alarming rasp of difficult breathing. On a chair nearby lay a shabby kilt and shirt, looking as though they had been hastily discarded.

Suspecting she was really stalling for time, she whispered, 'I'd better try again, Jamie, just in case.' Averting her eyes, she pushed the chair with its pile of clothing to one side, so she could bend nearer his father. 'Mr Murray!' she raised her voice, 'can you hear me?'

'He wakens straight away whenever I want him.' Again Jamie tugged at the robe she wore, this time more fiercely. 'Why won't you believe me?'

'I'm sorry.' Nervously Thea straightened, trembling slightly. 'I'll do what I can,' she promised helplessly, unwilling to confess that she didn't know where to begin. Jamie's anxious eyes reproaching her, stirred immediate sympathy, but as near as this she found his father even more intimidating, and unlike Jamie she knew he wouldn't appreciate her being here, if he woke up.

Yet, as she stared at him, an instinctive desire to help became uppermost. This man was obviously very ill, in need of someone. Young as he was, Jamie had taken her in. This could be one way of repaying such open hospitality. If only she could keep her strange agitation under control she might remember what little she knew about nursing.

'I think,' she glanced at Jamie, who waited tensely, 'your father should be covered up. The room's too cold. Isn't there a fire? Even an electric one would help. We could switch it on at once.'

Jamie shook his head. 'We don't have electric fires, they're too expensive to run. There's a fireplace, though.' He pointed to what looked to Thea like a great hole in the wall. 'But I'm not allowed to light fires.'

Thea considered the fireplace with frowning resignation. 'If you can show me where you keep your fuel, I'll see if I can get one going.' Suddenly the years she had spent in the same house as her ailing grandfather came back to her. While she hadn't been expected to nurse him, she must have absorbed how it was done? And she had helped with Gran, when she had been so ill, near the end.

Eager to get on with the fire, she quickly pulled up the rumpled blankets, startled, as she did so, to notice that Mr Murray's back was wet. He was steaming like a furnace, in spite of the coldness of the room.

It might be necessary to swab him down, she realised, wondering how this was to be done. Another frown touched her brow as she considered the build of him. How to turn him over? His pillows were damp and must be uncomfortable, yet again came the odd reluctance to see his face. This, being mixed with the even more curious desire to see it, had Thea biting her lip uncertainly.

Then she gasped as the choice was roughly taken from her, as with a low spate of unintelligible words Mr Murray flung himself forcibly over on to his back.

Jamie gave a small cry of fright and Thea found herself gulping. As if her breast was encased in iron she found she couldn't breathe. Her hands curled tightly in her palms and her eyes widened with unguarded fascination. Never could she remember seeing such an arresting face. For all Mr Murray was haggard, his cheeks sunken and like his body, damp with sweat, this didn't hide the hard handsomeness of his features. Awkwardly she started back, as though struck. In his present condition, which she suspected was some kind of 'flu or high fever, it would be difficult to guess how old he was, but he didn't look more than thirty-five or six. What a fool she had been to imagine he would be older! A tremor, so unknown and disturbing as to be unwelcome, began somewhere inside her, for all her slight body was almost rigid with surprise.

It took Jamie's anxious query to bring her back to reality. 'He's going to get well, isn't he?'

'I'm sure of it,' she murmured without conviction, dragging her eyes from the sick man's dark ravaged face. 'But we'd better try to light a fire as soon as possible. It's much too cold in here.'

She couldn't think now how she got it all done. A little

later she was feeling happier about some things but worse about others. It was only with the greatest difficulty that she had managed to get the fire going at all. For her it had proved far from easy, and she had been filled with terrible dread, on contemplating the enormous chimney, that it might be stuffed with jackdaws' nests, all of which might descend on top of her! Worse still, if the soot came down, or it smoked, it wouldn't do Mr Murray much good. It annoyed her, as it seemed a tangible sign of inefficiency, that before she got a good blaze going she was covered in soot herself. She was forced to borrow another of Mr Murray's dressing-gowns and had to leave him to go and change into it.

While the room warmed up, more to satisfy Jamie than from any real good she thought it might do, she bathed his father's face and hands. She couldn't understand why, as she touched the man, her senses should react as they did. Her heart began beating unevenly and a kind of prickling awareness attacked her limbs. It must be some kind of antagonism, the chemistry inside her rejecting that of his.

It was so strong it had astonished her that he had shown no sign of response. Contrarily, her nervous, slightly clumsy movements appeared to soothe him. As she ran a soft, cool cloth gently over his heated skin he almost ceased his restless mutterings and lay still. He still burned like a furnace, but he did stop tossing and turning—which appeared to convince Jamie that there was some improvement, after all.

Taking advantage of this temporary lull, Thea had covered him up again, unable to view with any equanimity the broad, bare expanse of his chest. After tucking his blankets in firmly, she had taken a tired Jamie downstairs and made him supper. It wasn't much but was all she could find, two eggs and a small tin of beans. He had looked quite surprised when she presented him with two eggs, as if he wasn't usually allowed so many, but he said nothing and ate them hungrily up.

It wasn't until after he had gone to bed that she realised she hadn't asked where he slept. Or where she might, should she ever get a chance! Perhaps for this one night she could sleep down here. The kitchen mightn't be particularly comfortable, but it was warm. Stifling a yawn, she made herself a cup of tea. Tomorrow she would leave. She must have been incredibly foolish to have come here in the first place.

CHAPTER TWO

SLOWLY Thea washed up Jamie's supper dishes and her own empty cup. Soon she must go back upstairs to see to Mr Murray, but she felt so helpless when there was so little she could do for him. She could bathe his brow and keep the fire going, but what he should have was proper medical attention; even someone with as little real knowledge of illness as herself could see that.

Unable to find anything in the way of medicine, she sliced up some lemons from the vegetable rack. Adding sugar, she poured boiling water over them. By the time she reached his room, along all those icy corridors, the drink should be cool. It had been one of Gran's favourite cold cures—if this was all Mr Murray was suffering from. Somehow Thea doubted it. She could have heated him some soup, but there didn't appear to be any in tins, and he was probably too ill to want anything, anyway.

Which was just as well, she decided dryly, as there was precious little food of any kind to be found in the larder. Perhaps he kept it under lock and key, only doling it out, as he thought necessary, in conjunction with all the other niggling little economies he seemed to be making of lighting, furniture and fuel.

Wearing her indignation like an armour, against she knew not what, Thea picked up her jug of lemon and marched angrily from the kitchen. Again she resolved to leave at dawn. There were bound to be more comfortable places in which to nurse her hurt feelings.

Mr Murray was still lying quietly where she had left him when she returned to his room. Immediately she noticed the room was warming up nicely and felt quite pleased with herself. She must remember, though, to bring up more logs. It was a longish haul from the kitchen, but the fire mustn't be allowed to go out.

Cautiously she approached the bed. Although he was quiet he still seemed very hot. Putting down the bowl of fresh water which she had collected as she passed the bathroom, she began bathing his face again. Now that she had her feelings under strict control, she didn't find this so difficult. It was simply a matter of being sensible, of reminding herself that Mr Murray was a sick man in need of help, and she, unfortunately, was the only one available to give it to him. He might have a wife and brothers, but none of them appeared to be here.

It obviously still soothed him when she bathed his face and hands, but she didn't like the way he repeatedly threw off his blankets. It couldn't be helping his fever and she continued to find it disturbing. Once, as she was pulling his sheets up, he opened his eyes and stared at her. It was a terrible shock, a curious experience. His eyes were like Jamie's, but a darker green. With a strangled little gasp she shrank from him, until she realised he wasn't really seeing her.

As he closed his eyes again her breathing returned to normal. Green eyes, a hard, handsome face and black hair. He was attractive, and she hated to think she was aware of it. Wasn't it high time she developed better judgment? Jerry had been a rogue, and while this man might not be that, he was married. After Jerry she had vowed she would never be taken in by a man again, yet here she was trembling because a perfect stranger had chanced to glance at her. An unconscious one, at that!

It was unforeseeable, of course, that just as she was deciding to leave him, Mr Murray should start shivering, and immediately her own problems fled as she found herself concentrating on his. First he was raging hot, now he was cold, for all the room was warmer. If she could find a pyjama jacket and get him into it, this might help.

Feeling she was trespassing, she opened several drawers but could find nothing, the vast majority of them being empty. Next she looked in the huge wardrobes, but without success. It puzzled her that the lady's wardrobe was completely empty and there were no women's clothes in the other one which contained only Mr Murray's suits.

Eventually she settled for one of his soft silk shirts, but when she tried nervously to get it around his broad shoulders he flung her off with such ferocity that she went flying back over the room. Unable to do anything to save herself, she banged her head on the side of the dressing-table and for a few moments she could see nothing but stars.

When the room righted itself again, with a soft moan she sat up. Nursing her sore head in her hands, she felt sure her neck must be broken. It took a lot of effort to scramble to her feet and return to the bed. Effort and courage! About to tell Mr Murray exactly what she thought of him, she saw hazily that he was still unconscious and couldn't have known what he was doing.

She went to sit on the bare carpet by the fire to recover, tears beginning to trickle down her cheeks, and she just sat there, letting them. It must be the silliest situation on earth —a girl like herself attempting to take care of a man like that! If she had been a real nurse it mightn't have been so crazy, but she wasn't. She had flown from London to escape what she had considered an intolerable situation and seemed well on her way to getting involved in another even worse one. With only a little more force Mr Murray might easily have done her a serious injury. She could still feel the almost frightening strength of his arms.

Deciding there was nothing more she could do for him but keep the room warm, she roused herself and went downstairs for more logs. With these she replenished the fire, grateful that the crackle of them disguised his difficult breathing. The fire grew hot, making her drowsy. She

must have fallen asleep as she woke with a start to hear
him mumbling again and throwing himself about. Fearing
he might fall out of bed, she jumped clumsily to her feet
and ran to his side.

'Mr Murray,' she implored, hoping she might get
through to him, 'you mustn't do that! You'll only make
yourself ill ...' Pausing helplessly, she substituted a hasty
'worse'. He was still very ill, she could see, although he
was cooler. She discovered this when she grasped his shoulder, in an automatic attempt to prevent him hurting himself.

She was completely unprepared when his arms shot out
and she found herself jerked swiftly down to him, toppled
on to the bed and held fast against his long, lean body.

'Let me go—at once!' she heard herself crying, her
breath almost removed by shock. 'Please, Mr Murray!'

She sensed at once that it was no good trying to reason
with him. He was delirious, possessing the extra strength of
someone temporarily out of their mind. He didn't know
what he was doing or saying, and she would be wiser to
save her breath to fight him. Words could be a sheer waste
of time.

Fright prompted her to begin hitting out at him, as
strangely, she seemed to be attacked both by him and the
wildest of feelings—feelings she found difficult to understand as they swept through her slight body. Fiercely she
tried to keep on fighting him, but the determined grip of
his arms made this more impossible by the minute.

Soon she was lying weakly panting, held fast against the
hard muscles of his broad chest. Fear mounted within her
as she lay half crying, not knowing what to do. Jamie might
come if she could manage to shout for help, but she was
reluctant to do this. He had so little, but he obviously
thought the world of his father. How could she risk strip-
ping that eager hero-worship from his eyes? She had an

uneasy feeling this might happen if he came in and found his father holding her like this.

No—she moved her head hopelessly, under the pressure of Murray's hand. She should have guessed what could happen and been prepared for it. With a little foresight such a situation might have been avoided, so it must be up to her to get herself out of it, without frightening Jamie.

Mr Murray's arms were still tightly around her and she was gathering strength to renew her struggles when she heard him muttering the first intelligible words he had said since she came. 'Kay,' she made out, 'I can't believe you've come back.'

'I haven't—you're crazy!' Terror coursed rigorously through Thea as she tried futilely to escape him. His voice was slurred, his harsh query resulting directly from inflamed lungs and mind. 'Please!' she entreated, hoping desperately to get through to him before he crushed her to death. 'You don't know what you're saying, Mr Murray. I'm not Kay!'

'Kay,' he laughed harshly, 'my sweet bitch of a wife!'

As Thea shrank from his contemptuous tones, she realised that her protests had done nothing more than stir his memory. Kay must be his wife and it seemed very clear that they were either separated or not on the best of terms. He sounded as though he would like to do something violent to her.

Too late Thea became aware that this indeed must be his intention. Without warning he turned on his side, pulling her closer, bringing his mouth down hard on hers. Shock and something else flared within her again as he crushed her lips beneath his. She tried to draw away, to protest, but the parting of her lips only served to inflame him more. Swiftly he seemed consumed by a devouring anger which threatened to send her into dark oblivion. Under the weight of his body and the force of his mouth she was held immobile.

She had never been kissed like this before. His body seemed a mass of throbbing need which quickly conveyed a message to hers. Against her will, while her mind only wanted to be free of him, every nerve, every fibre of her being started to respond. As his kiss deepened, becoming more demanding, she felt herself clinging to him, even when his main purpose appeared to be to inflict pain. This he was making abundantly clear, both with his mouth and in the hands that roamed brutally over her. Savagely he thrust the robe she wore aside, so that his hands might better explore her slender young body.

Praying feverishly that she wasn't going to faint, Thea tried to free herself, but as her hands caught in the roughness of his chest a burning sensation swept over her. It was like a flood of fire, a rawness of passion, bringing to her heart and limbs a kind of fluid awareness. Without her realising it was happening, her body went weak, from sensations she hadn't known existed. Suddenly, unbelievably, she felt herself relaxing, her mouth becoming almost as urgent as his.

The swiftness of her release was so unexpected, it kept her still for several seconds in sheer surprise. Dazed, she opened emotion-laden eyes to hear him gasp as he abruptly shook his head. While gulping air into her own deprived lungs, she saw him rub his hand over his eyes, as if trying desperately to wipe away the veil of darkness that blinded him.

'You've changed, Kay,' he said thickly. 'You make me want you.' Then his threatening attitude slowly changed. With all the inconsistency of a very sick man, he pushed her away and fell exhausted back on to his pillows.

Unable to speak, feeling terribly weakened by the experience she had just been through, Thea stumbled from the bed, across the room. As she left him, Mr Murray opened his eyes and looked straight at her, again without really seeing her. Fervently she hoped that when he did regain proper consciousness, he would remember nothing of her, or of what had just taken place.

Re-tying her robe with shaking fingers, she felt so upset she was forced to go to the bathroom for a drink of water, and was almost afraid to go back to the bedroom. Afterwards, she found it difficult to believe, after what had happened, that throughout the remainder of the night she had continued to tend the fire and look after the sick man.

Unable to understand why she found it impossible to leave him, she bathed his face and gave him sips of the diluted lemon. She took care, of course, not to get too near him, or when she had to she was careful to keep a wary eye on those strongly muscled arms. Her new sense of personal involvement was confusing, but she would only have herself to blame if the same thing happened again.

Why had his wife left him? she wondered, the empty wardrobe and neglected house no longer a mystery. Were they divorced, or had his wife simply got tired of living with a penny-pinching husband? Murray, Thea decided, was the kind of man who married the beautiful and sophisticated kind of woman. But some women, especially ones like that, often demanded luxury, deeming it more important than the most superior of men.

Staring down at him, as she now appeared to be doing with increasing frequency, she was conscious that she was becoming too concerned over both him and his son. Her compassion for Jamie she could tolerate, but never for his father. Not after the way he had kissed her, even if he hadn't known what he was doing. She shivered to think what could have happened if his fever weakened body hadn't denied him the fulfilment of the desires which, inexperienced as she was, she sensed had been moving within him.

As the fever slowly left him she thought his unconsciousness changed to a more natural sleep. But it wasn't until after six in the morning, when she awakened from an exhausted catnap in a chair, that she found him watching her.

'Who are you?' he asked abruptly, all traces of fever washed from his eyes as they met her tired ones. 'I could still be having hallucinations, of course. Maybe you don't really exist?'

So he didn't recognise her! He had no recollection of her looking after him or anything else? Coolly she tried to meet his enquiring gaze, knowing suddenly that she could never match this man in anything. Whatever she attempted to do, or think, he would always be one step ahead of her. This knowledge on top of what she had already suffered at his hands was almost too much. She might easily say something she would live to regret if she didn't have time to pull herself together. Closing her grey eyes defensively against the icy green of his, she made an abortive bid to do just that.

It proved a futile exercise. As though relentlessly bent on making her talk, he said thinly, 'If you were a naiad or a witch from the bogs of the moor, I could understand your silence.'

'How do you know I'm not, Mr Murray?' Her eyes flew open again as she challenged him flatly, 'Your mind might be still playing you tricks.'

This, curiously enough, seemed to startle him as his eyes narrowed and his powerful shoulders stiffened against the mound of pillows she had stuffed behind his back. 'Have I been out long?' He spoke as if he was quite familiar with the fever which had laid him low.

'I don't know how long.' She pushed back her long fair hair which had tangled in sleep about her shoulders. Uncertainly she got to her feet. 'I've only been here since last night. You were ill then, but how long before that I don't know. Jamie didn't say.'

'Jamie?' His mouth tightened and he ran his hand over

his forehead, in a gesture which was becoming familiar. 'Is
he all right?'

'I think so.'

'For God's sake, girl, answer me!'

'Mr Murray,' looking very young and indignant, Thea
tilted her chin, 'you have no call to speak to me like that!'

'Women invite it. You seldom give a straight answer to
a straight question.'

'As far as I know your son's in bed.'

Murray's eyes darkened with harsh anger. 'If I was capable of leaving this bed, I would shake you, madam, or put
you over my knee. I think the latter would be more in keeping with your age.'

What age would he have judged her to be through the
night, when he had forcibly kissed her? Would he have
judged her response that of a child? Her cheeks suddenly
hot, Thea thought not. 'You don't realise——' she began
to protest.

'What I do realise,' he cut in ruthlessly, 'is more than
enough. I come to, to find a complete stranger in my room,
sitting in front of a fire which I certainly didn't light, and
no sign of my son. Do you think I'm being unreasonable in
demanding an explanation? If you do then I must be going
out of my mind.'

'You have been.' She felt guilty for allowing herself a
little satisfaction over that. He was so authoritative he
would naturally hate any blank spaces in his life, when he
wasn't wholly aware of what he was saying or doing. Yet a
frown replaced her moment of triumph as she watched
him shifting impatiently. She could never hope to fight
him. Even in bed he looked superior. But, perversely, this
didn't prevent her reiterating with unwonted relish, 'Right
out of your mind!'

His dark face hardened aloofly. 'Don't enjoy yourself
too much at my expense. The boot could soon be on the
other foot.'

Thea's quick temper flared. 'There's no need for sarcasm, Mr Murray, or threats. Let me tell you, if it hadn't been for me you wouldn't have recovered nearly so quickly.'

'I suppose angels of mercy usually blow their own trumpets.'

'Better than sitting in heaven playing a harp, as you might have been doing if I hadn't been here,' she retorted sharply, although she doubted if Mr Murray, with his black visage, would have gone in that direction. 'You really needed me.'

'Your opinion?' he dismissed it indifferently. 'I've weathered other bouts of malaria without having my hand held.'

Immediately, because she wondered what he would say if she confessed that worse had happened than that, her face flooded with colour and she turned her head away.

'So that was too near the bone?' His eyes glittered on her averted face. 'One of these minutes—or will it be days —you might be willing to tell me exactly what you've been up to. And, incidentally, your name!'

This was too much! She could take contempt and ridicule, if it was deserved and fair, but downright ingratitude was something else again! Her cheeks still hot, she turned and marched to the bed, forgetting she wore only his dressing-gown which flapped about her feet, unfortunately detracting from the dignified approach she had hoped to make.

'My name is Andrews,' she said coldly, 'Thea Andrews. I didn't expect gratitude, Mr Murray, not even for spending the last twelve hours running up and down stairs, with logs for the fire I managed to light. Or for bathing your face and giving you drinks of water, which you couldn't have managed yourself. But I don't think I deserve insults!'

His mouth curled as his eyes went insolently over her, taking in her slim young body, the high curves of her agitated breasts. Her lengthy comments didn't appear to have impressed him. 'Women enjoy ministering to a man when he's helpless, but they'd run a mile when he's not. I expect you're no different from the rest. Decide what I owe you— you obviously think it a lot, and we'll bring it down to terms of hard cash.'

Thea shuddered away from his all-seeing glance, a glance which seemed to be making her aware of things she hadn't been personally aware of before. It had been the same when he had held her in his arms.

Jerking her mind from this, she retorted quickly, 'You've already repaid me with a lump on my head, along with other things, when you flung me across the room.'

A frown creased his brow, flickering through his eyes. 'What made me do that?'

As though it had been her fault! 'I was simply trying to tidy your blankets.' She decided not to mention the shirt and give him more cause to jeer.

'Because you couldn't bear the sight of me with nothing on?'

She tried to keep cool, to pretend indifference to such sarcastic taunts, which she suspected were born more from frustration than anything else. Outside there must be plenty of work for him to do if, as Jamie had said, they had practically no staff. Having to lie here, waiting to recover, would never suit a man like this.

'Well?' he prompted.

She took a deep breath. 'This is a bedroom, Mr Murray, not a beach.'

'Two places where clothes aren't always necessary,' he rejoined sardonically, 'although you sound prim enough to be wearing Victorian nightgowns. Oh . . .' with an impatient groan he fell back, 'my damned head!'

In alarm, Thea touched his arm, her eyes appealing. 'Please calm down. You'll only make yourself ill again, asking a lot of silly questions.'

His eyes hard with dislike, he stared up at her. 'Can't

you get it into your head that I'm not asking silly questions! I want to know what you're doing here—why you're in my room, wearing my dressing-gown, and have apparently been given, or taken, the freedom of my house. I won't always be sick. I don't happen to be a permanent invalid, so disabuse yourself of that idea. In a few hours' time I'll be on my feet and quite able to remove you from my premises, unless you can produce a suitable explanation.'

'I certainly have one!' Yet her indignation was lost in a sudden urge to soothe him, a mysterious desire she found difficult to account for. She had a suspicion that she would rather see him arrogantly demanding than helpless. 'I'll tell you all you want to know,' she promised recklessly, 'but wouldn't you like a cup of tea or something first? It wouldn't take me long to make one, and you might feel better afterwards.'

'Later,' he conceded, not giving an inch, although his face was grey again and damp with sweat. Grimly his eyes queried her reluctance. 'Well, I'm waiting.'

Suddenly she decided to say nothing of her original intention of staying here as a paying guest, nor of being born at Drumlarig and remaining here with her mother. 'I'm looking for a job, actually,' this had been what she had intended doing, after she'd had a look around. 'I saw your advertisement for a housekeeper, at the end of your road.'

His green eyes narrowed, she hoped it wasn't with suspicion. It was. 'That doesn't ring quite true, somehow,' he said softly. 'My road is too far off the beaten track. It couldn't be an accident that you were there in the dark.'

Thea gulped, racking her brains quickly, discovering that even the smallest lie couldn't be told easily, at least not by a novice like herself. 'I heard someone talking about it, in the village I came through. Then I asked the way to Drumlarig.' The last bit was the truth, at any rate.

'Whom did you ask?'

'A man. I don't know his name.'

This only appeared to make him more sceptical, but he seemed to dismiss it as unimportant. 'So you arrived here and Jamie let you in. He shouldn't have done.'

Quickly she sprang to the defence of the absent boy. 'That's surely irrelevant, Mr Murray. He's only a child, after all, and he was frightened. I think he would have been pleased to see anybody.'

Murray went on, as though she had never spoken, 'Nor should he have brought you up here.'

'He wasn't going to until I told him I'd had nursing experience. Don't you appreciate how worried he is about you?'

'Do you have nursing experience, Miss Andrews?'

Stiffening resentfully at his tone, Thea muttered, 'What's the good of asking questions if you aren't going to believe what I say?'

Looking her over again, he shrugged. 'We're both wasting our time. You're much too young for the post of housekeeper.'

'Really, Mr Murray, is that fair?' But knowing her age to be against her, she hurried on to point out other things. 'You do need someone and you aren't likely to get another applicant. Not many women would care to bury themselves in an isolated spot like this. The house alone is——' she had been about to say, terrible, but the angle of his jaw warned her in time, 'beautiful but inconvenient,' she improvised quickly, 'And I'm sure I've proved how capable I am.'

'How old are you?'

Dared she tell another? 'Twenty-nine,' she answered rashly. 'I've always looked young for my age, but I'm almost thirty.'

'I'd never have thought it,' he returned dryly, but thankfully she saw he was still too weak for forceful argument. 'You're English, of course?'

'Is that still a crime in Scotland, Mr Murray?'

'No, but your tongue is. It's too sharp.'

It might be, she was ready to admit, but only when provoked. 'I'm usually quite cheerful and good-tempered, but I do believe in free speech.'

'Please feel free to say what you like—until I leave this bed,' he finished silkily.

Thinking she might be wiser not to comment on that, she asked hurriedly, 'Does this mean I'm—er—hired?'

'Engaged?' The faint twitch of his lips might have been amusement over her choice of words. 'For a trial period only. You'll have to prove satisfactory, and there's a lot more I'll need to know before I'd even think of taking you on permanently. That might have to wait for a day or two, though.' The amusement faded from his mouth as it tightened, as if his weakened condition angered him.

'I'll make sure you have no cause for complaint,' Thea hastened humbly, in what she hoped was the appropriate manner.

'Just as long as you don't start making them,' he rejoined sarcastically. 'The others all did.'

Silently watching his renewed efforts to sit up, Thea wondered doubtfully if she had done the right thing. At least she would have a roof over her head until she had decided what she really wanted to do. Nothing could be worse, surely, than walking around the countryside in this weather? She hadn't realised it would be so bad. Being part of a busy household might take her mind off her own problems until she was ready to sort them out. The ten years she had added to her age could be a bit of a nuisance, but before Murray had time to take a good look at her, if he ever did, she might be able to do something about that.

That he had to forsake his attempts to sit up didn't, she noticed, improve his temper. Sweat, because of his weakened condition, began beading his broad forehead, but instinct warned her against attempting to wipe it off, as she had done through the night. Unconscious, he had managed to scare her half out of her wits. Now, while he was fully aware of what he was doing, she felt even more apprehensive, although she couldn't say exactly why. It must be because of his bare expanse of chest which, as yet, he had made no attempt to cover up.

It startled her that he seemed to know what she was thinking and was amused by it. Again his mouth curved in faint derision. 'If you wouldn't mind returning my dressing-gown, Miss Andrews, the sight of me might not offend you so much. Although I shouldn't have thought a girl with nursing experience would have found the sight of a little bare skin alarming!'

They were staring at each other, Murray very hard and decisive, Thea with a hot flush over her cheeks, a sudden, unpredictable antagonism seeming to hurl them together. It was almost more than she could manage to tear her eyes away.

Looking down at the dressing-gown as an excuse, she tried to explain, 'I had to borrow it last night as I was wet through, but I'll go and see if my own clothes are dry yet. Then I can bring your tea.'

'No hurry.'

Well, that sounded reasonable. Encouraged, she glanced at him again. 'Could you tell me where I can find Jamie? He took himself off to bed without showing me where his room is.'

'I think you'll find him in the kitchen, as it's almost seven. You might tell him I can't take him to school this morning.'

'Then what will he do?'

'He can walk.'

'But it's miles!' she had to protest at such a harsh decision. Poor Jamie!

'There's a short cut through the fields, Miss Andrews.'

Thea hesitated, fearing she might be wasting her breath. 'Would you mind if I took him, Mr Murray? I do drive.'

'You have a licence?'

'Yes.' Did he have to make it so obvious that he didn't believe her?

'The river will still be up if it hasn't stopped raining. Can you manage a Land Rover?'

'I've had some experience.'

He raised his eyebrows. 'Just make sure you take extra care when you go through the ford, with Jamie beside you.'

His tone, indicating that it wouldn't bother him if she drowned in the ford if she were by herself, enraged her, but before she could comment, he turned over and closed his eyes. The brief strength he had found to talk to her had gone. Feeling dismissed, Thea placed a few more logs on the smouldering fire and quietly left the room.

There followed one of the most hectic mornings she had ever known, but strangely, for all she was so busy, she couldn't remember ever feeling so exhilarated. Her grandmother had taught her that it was good for a girl to be useful as well as educated, and Thea had dutifully learnt a lot about running a house. But she had always been over-protected and had never known what it was to have to scrimp and save. Perhaps, at Drumlarig, she felt good because at long last she was getting a chance to stand on her own two feet. Not even Jerry's duplicity seemed to hurt so much this morning.

She suspected, however, that the source of her newly found optimism sprang not so much from this as from the mysterious sense of homecoming which seemed to increase with every hour. Nowhere did she feel a stranger. Every door she opened held more or less what she expected. Even outside, where she was escorted by an eager Jamie in the dawn light, many of the paths seemed familiar.

She couldn't remember people, not even old Martha, who had apparently lived at Drumlarig all her life, so must have been here when Thea was born. Martha was a widow

whose husband had been dead for many years. Her health
being bad, she could only help when she was able, which
wasn't often. For this, she informed Thea, she received her
keep and a small wage.

Jamie, fast losing his reserve, ate a good breakfast. He
had shown Thea the warm, straw-covered barn where the
big brown hens laid their eggs, and she had scrambled him
two for his breakfast. She had piled them high in mounds
on fresh-made toast, spread with lots of golden butter, as
she couldn't find any bacon. The larder proved even less of
an Aladdin's cave, this morning, than it had done the
previous evening.

When she asked Jamie why there was no bacon, he just
shook his head. It was Martha who replied that they
couldn't afford such luxuries, that Himself wasn't made of
money. Thea said nothing more, her last encounter with
Murray making her instinctively cautious, but her list of
mental notes was growing. There were things she vowed
she would have out with him, once he was well again and
she was firmly established.

She watched Jamie finish off his milk and, when he asked
if he could have some more, she filled up his glass. When
Martha grumbled that if he drank all the milk there would
be none left to make cream for butter, Thea took no notice.
After he had finished, she told him to run upstairs and say
goodbye to his father, then get his school satchel.

While he was gone, Martha continued to grumble over
the milk. It was quite clear that she considered Thea was
taking too much upon herself too soon. 'I used to do the
milking,' she finished, on a less aggressive note, 'but now I
can't because of my rheumatism. Mr Logan does it these
days, but he won't be able to again until he's better, which
mightn't be until this afternoon.'

'This afternoon!' Thea thought the old woman must
have taken leave of her senses. 'Why, he isn't fit to be out

of bed! After I take Jamie to school I'm going to find a doctor.'

'You'll get no thanks for it! Mr Logan knows what's wrong with him. It's this foreign fever.'

'I don't know what it is, but I can see he's very ill. If the worst comes to the worst,' Thea promised rashly, 'I'll milk the cow myself!'

'You?' Martha was taken aback. 'Where did a girl like you learn to milk?'

'On a farm,' Thea replied evenly. She had, in fact, often passed the long weeks between school terms helping an elderly couple on a nearby farm. She couldn't have forgotten everything the Freemans had taught her.

Unimpressed, Martha sniffed. 'If you once take it on, you might get landed with it for good. Never say I didn't warn you.' When Thea remained silent, she shot her another glance out of sharp brown eyes. 'I never thought Mr Logan would ever take on someone like you as a housekeeper, although I don't suppose you'll last long. Six, he's had, in the last few years.'

'Six!'

Smugly, Martha nodded. 'I thought that would surprise you! I could tell you all their names, if you doubt me. None of them stayed more than a week or two.'

Hastily declining Martha's offer, Thea took a deep breath, asking impulsively, 'What about Mr Murray's wife?'

Martha replied shortly, her tone betraying a reluctance to talk of it, 'She's dead, and good riddance. She never was the wife for him, and he knew it.'

The woman's remarks were so frank, Thea felt shocked. She wouldn't have felt surprised to have heard that Murray had murdered his wife, with Martha as a willing accomplice. Through the night he had sounded as though he'd hated her. Martha, apparently, hadn't liked her either, but then Martha would be hard to please.

'I'm sorry.' Rather helplessly she stared at Martha, not knowing quite what to say. 'Jamie must be very lonely sometimes.'

'Aye, and Himself, too,' Martha rejoined soberly. 'Mr Logan needs a woman, but I don't think he will ever marry again. Mind you, there are those who would like to make him change his mind, the widow of his late brother being one of them, but I doubt if any of them will succeed.'

CHAPTER THREE

IF Martha had given her food for thought, it was a while before Thea had time to ponder over what she had learnt. After taking Jamie to the village she dropped him off at his school, then, going back the same way as she had come, she called at the doctor's house, which Jamie had pointed out to her.

The doctor was out, but she left word with his daughter, stressing how important it was that her father called at Drumlarig as soon as possible. Mr Murray, she said, was very ill.

The doctor's daughter, a tall, dark girl, studied Thea curiously, with a hint of alarm in her face. She didn't ask any questions, however, she simply promised that the doctor would get Thea's message.

The Land Rover, Thea discovered, was much the same as the Range Rover which her grandfather had owned when they had lived in the country. She hadn't explained to Logan Murray that she had learnt to drive in the Range Rover, that she had driven it for miles over quiet estate roads. As it had stopped raining, the water at the ford was shallow and she had little trouble in getting across.

She could see this morning that she had been wrong in her previous estimation. What she had thought was merely a stream, and Jamie had referred to as a burn, was in reality exactly what Logan Murray had called it, a river—a fairly narrow one, it was true, but definitely a river. Thea had a hollow feeling inside her at the thought of what might have happened if she had fallen into it when it was deeper. With just a little more rain to swell it, it might easily have been a raging torrent, strong enough to sweep her away.

She drove fast, the thought of Logan Murray being alone in the house and ill troubling her. She might never come to like the man, not after the way he had treated her during the night, to say nothing of his curtness this morning, but she would hate to think she couldn't feel normal human pity. Martha might sound as if she worshipped the ground Mr Logan walked on, but she didn't seem very keen to do much to help him. If he was unconscious again he might easily have fallen out of bed?

Logan. Logan Murray! Suddenly it came to Thea that this must be the same Logan Murray who had obligingly stood by her years ago while she had had her photograph taken. Why it hadn't really registered until now she couldn't think. It must have been because of the more startling things she had been listening to regarding his wife. Ruefully she supposed that the long years and an ill-fated marriage must have changed him. The vague remembrance she had of him as a youth, gentle and kind, didn't somehow fit in with the man he was today, ruthlessly hard and dangerously masculine.

Would—could an unhappy marriage alone so harden a man? Martha had insinuated that the marriage hadn't been happy, and certainly Logan's own remarks would back this up, but surely Jamie was living evidence that Logan Murray and his wife hadn't always been so estranged? She wondered how long his wife had been dead, how she had died. She couldn't have been so very old.

Other things puzzled Thea as she drove carefully through the ford again before putting on speed for the remaining distance to the house. Martha had spoken of a brother's widow, which must mean that Logan had lost a brother as well. And what of his parents? When she and her mother had left Drumlarig they had both been alive.

Thea sighed as she drew up too quickly outside the front door, impatient of her own feelings. What had happened at Drumlarig since she had lived here years ago was none of her business, and she was uneasily convinced that it wouldn't improve her relationship with Logan Murray if she were to try and make it so!

Remembering that the doctor would need room to park his car, she parked her own vehicle nearer the end of the house. After she had jumped out something made her glance up at the window above her. To her astonishment she thought she saw Murray standing there looking down on her, but when she blinked with dismay and looked up again he was gone. If he had ever been there. Yet she could have sworn she hadn't just imagined she had seen him.

Without going near the kitchen, she rushed straight upstairs. She had been right to worry. His fever must have returned. He must be delirious and wandering about his room this time. She was so anxious she forgot all about her resolve to try and make herself look older before he saw her again. As she neared his room she did wonder why she should feel such a sense of anxious urgency, but decided it must be because she had no wish to spend any longer than necessary nursing him.

Bursting into his bedroom, her hair flying, colour wildly tinting her breathless young face, she also forgot she was supposed to represent the cool efficiency of the nursing profession. 'Mr Murray!' she cried, her voice raised in disapproval even as she opened his door. Then, startled, she stopped short. He was in bed, not wandering about the room, lying quietly, although she knew with him this could be a deception. It was his expression that told her he was far from pleased about something.

'Miss Andrews?'

Before he could attack her, as he was so obviously about to, for entering his room in such an impetuous fashion, she beat him to it. 'You've been out of bed?' She had thought she might have been mistaken, now she wasn't so sure.

His voice was curt, leaving her very aware of his rising anger. 'I won't have you speaking to me like that, girl, and

I must repeat what I said earlier. If you want to work for me then I ask the questions.'

More from a sense of frustration than any real desire to annoy him, she retorted quickly, 'We're not living in the Dark Ages, Mr Murray! At least, I didn't think so until I came here! I'm quite aware that you probably intend sending me packing as soon as you're well again, but while I'm looking after you, I think I have the right to know why you've been out of bed.'

The glitter in his eyes was almost brilliant. 'You have no rights at all, Miss Andrews, when it comes to me. Neither you nor any other woman, remember that. I left this bed simply to test the strength of my legs and to see who was coming up the road too fast. I might have known it was you! In future, if you can't drive with more care, don't take any vehicle of mine out again.'

Sullenly, Thea stared at him, thinking he was full of arrogant ingratitude. 'Don't you understand it was because of you I was hurrying? Which should prove I do have a sense of responsibility.' Making a greater effort to ignore his ever curling lips, she asked politely, 'And how did you feel when you were out of bed?'

'Bloody awful,' he confessed, with tight-lipped impatience, 'but I can't afford to lie here.'

Thea's eyes fell away from his quickly. Perhaps there were things she couldn't afford to indulge in either. Did he have to look like some proud Highland chieftan, even when shirtless and in need of a shave? Shivering, she recalled the feeling of that rough, cleft chin against her soft flesh, the firm insistence of the mouth above it. Ill though he was, the rate he was making her heart beat was far from comfortable. It was imperative that by the time he was up and about she should have her emotions well under control. Something she might only achieve if she stopped thinking how she had felt when he had kissed her.

Meeting the glinting irritation in Murray's eyes, she said

sharply, 'You can't expect to feel up to much after what you've had. Or are still having,' she finished, with ill-concealed relish. She wasn't going to reassure him by saying she thought he seemed much better, nor would she sin by telling him he looked worse. He was too full of ingratitude and conceit of himself. After all she had done for him she had barely received a word of thanks!

To her alarm, he repeated her thoughts almost exactly. 'While you're busy counting all the things you've done for me, Miss Andrews, let me remind you, yet again, that you work for me. I might not have known about it myself, but you obviously had it all planned, from the moment you set foot in my house. You wanted to be my housekeeper. This being the case, you must have realised what such a position entailed.'

'You're hateful!'

The hard voice cut inexorably through her unconscious protest. 'Enough, Miss Andrews! If this is to be your opinion of me, voiced or otherwise, every time I give an order, then you may as well pack your bags—or did Jamie say a rucksack—and go. And at once!'

'Oh, no!' Her eyes widening with a startled dismay, Thea retreated in abject cowardice. 'I'm sorry, Mr Murray. I—I don't want to be sent away ...'

'Unless you're prepared to change your ways you will be,' he threatened remorselessly. 'And, believe me, I've seen too many so-called housekeepers come and go to be unduly disturbed at the prospect of losing yet another.'

She knew she had gone pale and her slight body shook as she went nearer the bed. Her hand went out imploringly to touch his, without fully realising what she was doing. 'I promise, Mr Murray,' her fingers tightened urgently, although she knew he could never understand why she wanted so desperately to stay here, 'I promise to do better.'

'As you did earlier,' he retorted cynically, his gaze transferring to the hand which still clutched his arm. 'Is this a promise of some future bonus for me, if I'm prepared to overlook the obvious—ah—vagaries of your temperament?'

Cheeks flushing scarlet, Thea snatched her hand away, bitterly regretting her too impulsive nature. In the last few weeks it had led her into plenty of trouble, surely she had learnt her lesson? 'I'm sorry,' she stammered, 'I—I didn't realise what I was doing.'

His regard was suddenly closer, more personal, as if he idly contemplated turning her impulsiveness to some future advantage. Then, apparently tiring of the conversation, he said less curtly, 'I have no particular desire to throw you back on to the roads at this time of year, but I won't warn you again. Did you manage to get Jamie safely to school?'

'Oh yes.' Her anxiety to placate him being stronger than the indignation she felt when he implied she was a homeless vagabond, she smiled faintly. 'He wasn't late, if that's what you're thinking.'

'It wasn't.'

Hastily, sensing Jamie meant a lot to him even if he was raising him in the most Spartan manner, she added, 'He's a nice little boy.' When Murray made no reply but continued looking at her, she changed the subject briskly. 'Now, can I get you anything?'

'You can get me a drink.'

'Whisky, you mean?' When he nodded with mock patience, she protested, 'It won't be good for you, I'm sure. Besides, the doctor's coming.'

She had called on the doctor for Murray's own good, but her heart sank as she saw his expression. 'You asked Stewart to come here?'

'Jamie said he was your doctor.'

Murray muttered something under his breath that she didn't catch. 'The telephone's out of order. You must have gone to his house. Never do that again, Miss Andrews!'

'I only saw his daughter.'

Again Murray's mouth compressed. 'Better and better,'

he observed cynically. 'I take it she was concerned?'

'Didn't you expect her to be? Or is that a naïve question?'

'I advised you to watch your step, miss!'

'Yes, I know.' She knew she had overstepped the mark. Hesitantly she dared, 'But you aren't very encouraging, Mr Murray.'

His mouth twisted, but not in a smile. 'Do you like your employers to be encouraging, Miss Andrews?'

Biting her lip with mortification, she turned quickly to replenish the fire, while not having the strength, she supposed, to follow up his cool taunts, he lapsed into silence.

The logs went on and there was a small pause until they caught hold, to crackle and spark against the dark hole of a chimney. Pushing at one of them with the toe of her boot, Thea was rewarded with a small burst of flame. The warmth was good on a cold December morning and she held out her hands to it gratefully. She didn't see Logan Murray noticing how the pale gold of her thick head of hair was reflected in the flames, and the way in which her delicately pure profile was etched against them.

As the silence grew so did a twinge of guilt. Logan Murray was right, her attitude as a servant was all wrong. She shouldn't be standing here, taking her ease before his fire, as though she was the lady of the house with nothing better to do. Reluctantly she returned to the bed. He had closed his eyes and his face was as grey as the dawn. The dressing-gown he had demanded lay discarded. He had pulled a sheet carelessly over the lower part of his body, but his broad shoulders and the top of his dark chest were still bare.

'Are you all right, Mr Murray?' she felt like a parrot, being sure she had asked him this a dozen times, without getting a proper answer.

She had guessed her slightly breathless voice might annoy him, but not how much. Opening his green eyes, he stared straight into hers, so she couldn't avoid seeing the dislike in his. 'Do you think I'd be lying here if I was?'

Ask a silly question! But did he have to be so intolerant? Every time she showed concern did he have to snap her head off? Unhappily she shook her head, avoiding his arrogant gaze. 'Haven't you got a pyjama jacket, Mr Murray? I mean, if the doctor's coming.'

'Haven't you got anything but a pair of jeans?' he countered, his eyes lowering to that part of her anatomy which her blue jeans covered too closely.

She didn't care for the way his glance lingered on her long, slender legs, the neat but provocative curves below her narrow waist. His glance had nothing suggestive about it, but it missed nothing. 'No—well——' she began, trying to get rid of the peculiar heat in her throat, a heat which also affected her suddenly trembling limbs.

He had no patience to wait until she could articulate clearly. 'It's no good looking for excuses,' he snapped, 'where none exist. I don't want any housekeeper of mine going around looking like a mixed-up teenager. In those you look about seventeen, instead of,' he frowned as he paused, 'did you say twenty-nine?'

Reluctantly she nodded her head this time. 'I understand. I'll see what I can find.'

'Well, get me that whisky.' He wasn't a man to soften his blows with a kind word in between.

Obediently Thea turned towards the cupboard where he told her he kept it. Logan Murray was a stranger, one she found impossible to recall from childhood memories. He had such a high-handed manner about him, such a curt enunciation that even his voice made her feel tense. No wonder he was so alone. Would any woman be able to cope with him?

Yet, as she watched fascinated as he swilled down more whisky than she thought good for him, she suspected there might be no shortage of women willing to take on the

master of Drumlarig. Logan Murray had a certain—appeal,
his looks and figure assured her of that. He also had a hard
vitality which not even his present illness could disguise.
To many women he might prove irresistible and Thea was
inclined to suspect that, if he felt like it, he wouldn't be
above amusing himself with them. But he might be capable of being utterly callous, her intuition warned, when
he tired of them.

'Now,' he said, the thump of the much depleted whisky
bottle startling her as he set it down, 'I might be able to
make the bathroom. If I can manage to shave it might be
enough to prevent Stewart sending for the undertaker.'

He had ignored the glass she had given him, drinking the
whisky straight from the bottle. Fascinated, she watched
him wipe his mouth with the back of his hand. 'Do you
really think you should go to the bathroom?' she began,
then paused, colour flooding her cheeks.

His brows rose ironically. 'For a girl—well, you're
scarcely that at twenty-nine—a woman, I should say, with
nursing experience, you seem unbelievably innocent!'

Equally unbelievably he appeared to be laughing at her!
A flare of temper replaced Thea's embarrassment. He didn't
have to endow everyone with the same level of experience
as himself! 'I'll get back to the kitchen, then, and see to
your lunch. I can't be in two places at once!' In a rather
muddled fashion, she attempted to escape with dignity, but
when he suddenly began throwing off his bedclothes she
took one apprehensive look at him and fled.

Doctor Stewart, who reminded Thea vaguely of the
older doctor in a TV series her grandmother had been fond
of watching, arrived an hour later. By this time she had
finished all the breakfast dishes and generally tidied up. It
hadn't been necessary to discover if she could still milk a
cow as Murray's shepherd arrived and said he would do
the inbye jobs. Which meant, he explained, when she asked

him, the tasks to be done around the steading and fields surrounding the house. He didn't seem too alarmed to learn that Logan was ill.

'I thought he might be, when he wasn't up on the hill this morning. He didn't look over grand yesterday.' Duncan only looked surprised when Thea told him she was the new housekeeper, but he merely nodded his head, making no verbal comment.

Martha explained that Duncan was the one man whom Murray employed, and he lived in an old farmhouse on the moors. On the rare occasion when Murray had 'the fever' Duncan always knew and came down. Such devotion seemed to Thea extraordinary. Did Duncan get paid, she wondered, or was he too expected to labour for next to nothing?

Forgetting that Murray had asked her to wear something more in keeping with her position, she went to meet the doctor, but was surprised to find him already halfway over the hall. She greeted him politely.

His thick, bushy brows shot up when he saw her and stayed there, instead of reverting to their natural position when she introduced herself. 'Dear me,' he muttered dryly, 'what did you say was the matter with him?'

Implying as he did that Murray's mind must be affected to have taken her on, Thea stared at the doctor coldly. 'I don't know what's the matter with him, doctor, but I believe he's quite ill, and I don't think he's much better this morning, although he's determined to get out of bed.'

'Yes, well,' Stewart hummed a little, 'he's not a man to stay there any longer than he can help, and that's a fact. We'll just have to see what we can do, won't we. I'll go up by myself, if you don't mind.'

A man of few words and an even more derogatory eye than Murray! For a moment Thea thought she had puzzled the doctor, but she couldn't be sure. She didn't seem to be making a very brilliant start. Obviously no one liked her being here very much. Only Jamie, and even his trust hadn't been fully won yet.

While the doctor was upstairs she began thinking about lunch and was again dismayed by the lack of ingredients. 'Will it be one of my jobs to buy the provisions?' she asked Martha, thinking she would soon have the larder shelves filled.

'Yes, but he will tell you how much you can spend.'

Thea digested this in silence. How devious! It was quite apparent that he would give her a small amount of money, then complain that she didn't shop economically. For that matter, could she? Never before had she had the responsibility of shopping for a family. Gran had always taken care of that, along with her housekeeper. Now that Thea was a housekeeper herself, she found herself wishing she had had more experience to draw on. During the few months, since Gran died and she had been on her own, she had just gone out and bought whatever she had wanted, without keeping any check on what she spent. And it must have cost her quite a packet, she realised ruefully, recalling the almost constant stream of people who had dropped in—her so-called friends, who had brought their friends!

Doctor Stewart rapped on the kitchen door on his way out. 'Your master will be better off in bed,' he addressed both Martha and Thea. 'Give him plenty of warm, nourishing drinks, not whisky, and see if you can keep him there.'

Because Doctor Stewart still eyed her disapprovingly, Thea retorted with a sharpness which would have earned an immediate rebuke from her grandmother. 'If Mr Murray doesn't want to stay in bed, I don't think I could make him. Not even if I sat on him!'

'I'm not asking you to do that, girl.'

Biting her lip, Thea went hot with embarrassment. What on earth had made her come out with anything so childish? The doctor wouldn't be impressed.

He obviously wasn't. Refusing a cup of tea which she contritely offered, he turned abruptly. 'If you should need me again get in touch. My daughter may call tomorrow. Good day to you both.'

After he had gone, Martha said nothing, as though there was nothing more to be said. Thea asked slowly, 'Does Miss Stewart come here often?'

'Whenever she can find an excuse, and sometimes without one.'

Thea regretted having asked. If she stayed it would be part of her duties, she supposed, to be pleasant to Logan Murray's friends when they called, so why should the thought of Miss Stewart calling be distasteful?

Quickly she reached for the kettle and filled it, trying to get rid of the memory of Logan's arms around her, his lips on hers. She couldn't possibly be feeling possessive about him, after only a few hours! Yet his kisses, even given unconsciously, had aroused curious emotions. When she closed her eyes she could still feel a kind of hot excitement swirling through her body, arousing a peculiar, unfamiliar yearning which she couldn't easily dismiss.

As she spooned tea into the pot, she found it hard to accept that Logan Murray wasn't impressed by her. It was much too late, but she wondered if it would have made any difference if she had been honest with him from the start. It must be her own fault that the opportunity had probably passed for ever. By coming here under false pretences, she might have made it impossible ever to tell him the truth.

For his lunch she wished she had had fish or a chicken, but she could find nothing like that. In the end she made him an egg custard which, as she was a naturally good cook, looked very nice. Confident of her ability in this sphere at least, she carried it up to him. The tray might look rather bare, but she had taken great pains over it.

'Take it away!' he groaned harshly, as she set it down

beside him. 'If you'd had any sense at all you'd have known I don't feel like eating anything.'

'It's all I could find,' she snapped back, hating him, 'but it will do you good.'

'Hand me that bottle of whisky,' Logan ordered, 'if you can find where that fool of a doctor's put it. It'll get me out of here faster than anything else.'

Thea didn't move, neither did she remove the tray. 'Doctor Stewart wouldn't approve, I'm sure.'

'You mean you don't?' He shot her a sour glance. When she didn't reply, he added coldly, 'John's a good enough doctor, but he should know better than to preach to me. He knows as well as I do that I haven't time to wait for the more conventional methods to work.'

'You mean you'd rather stick to the method you enjoy,' Thea rejoined, with a matching coldness. 'What's the good of having doctors if we aren't prepared to follow their advice?'

'You sent for him, Miss Andrews, not me, remember?' he retorted savagely. 'And I shouldn't set myself up as a virtuous teetotaller, if I were you, for you neither look the part of that or anything else.'

So this was what women meant when they talked of men being unlivable with when they were ill! She could see that Logan Murray was no exception. He was obviously in a smouldering, highly inflammable mood. Maybe if she tried to humour him?

'If Miss Stewart is coming to see you, she mightn't like it if the room's smelling of alcohol.'

As he was about to raise himself from his pillows, Thea saw him pause. 'No woman comes here, Miss Andrews, unless they're a servant, like yourself. I've had enough of women in my bedroom to last me a lifetime. They're not content just with a man's body, they want his soul.'

'That's none of my business!' Thea might have over-looked being called a servant, in such tones, but the intended insult behind it she could not. It was something she wouldn't forget in a hurry, even if for the moment she must. 'Speaking generally,' she exclaimed, thinking fleetingly of Jerry, 'men tend to over-estimate their own charms. Unless you were ill, Miss Stewart probably wouldn't dream of coming up here.'

His hand shot out and caught her arm. 'I've told you before, Miss Andrews, I don't need your opinion on every remark I pass. I hope you're right about Miss Stewart, but it she turns up this afternoon, then it's up to you to get rid of her.'

She tried to drag her arm free. His grip hurt, but the flickers of electricity worried her more. 'Is that all, Mr Murray?'

'It's not, but it will do for the time being.' He lay back again and alarmed by his pallor she stared at him, her antagonism momentarily gone. Instinctively she knew that the fever he suffered from had depleted his strength more than he liked, or would admit.

'What did the doctor say was wrong?' she heard herself asking, to her surprise, almost tenderly, in spite of the soreness of the arm he had just released.

'Nothing that I won't recover from very quickly, if I'm left in peace,' he finished grimly.

That afternoon when she collected Jamie from school a few flakes of snow fell against her windscreen. The sky was grey, but the glistening whiteness of the feathery flakes where they settled on the winter green of the fir-trees enchanted her. The Land Rover hadn't been going well and this seemed to more than make up for it.

'Look, Jamie,' she cried, 'snow for Christmas!' She laughed happily, expecting him to join in her sense of anticipation. Somehow, although this was her first day at Drumlarig, she found herself looking forward to spending Christmas here much more than she had done at St Moritz. Jamie would have a tree and she would help him to decorate it. She hadn't had one since they had left the country, and though she had pretended she hadn't missed it she did.

She tried to share a few of her childhood memories with Jamie, being careful to give no hint of the size and comfort of her grandfather's home.

'I've never had a Christmas tree.' Thea thought he sounded wistful behind his apparent indifference. 'I don't think my mother liked the mess they make and my father doesn't care for that sort of thing either. Nor does he like snow as it's bad for the stock and makes a lot of extra work.'

Poor little boy! Thea felt a positive surge of pity again. Between his two parents he seemed to have had a raw deal, and was still having one, if she was any judge of fathers. Her pride still stinging from Logan Murray's abrupt dismissal after lunch, as well as from his previous remarks, she had no hesitation in condemning him, in her own mind, as a man who ought never to have had children.

'Never mind,' deliberately she spoke lightly, glancing quickly at Jamie's uncertain face, 'this Christmas we'll have a tree. I'll get round your father, somehow.'

In the village shop she managed to purchase a bottle of barley water and other such beverages, together with some fruit and icecream, and more general items which they were short of. She kept the bill which she settled herself but intended presenting to Logan later. At the butcher's she bought some meat and a plump chicken along with some bones for soup. Here, too, she paid and kept the bill.

After picking Jamie up, while she was hunting through the box of groceries for a packet of sweets she had got for him, he drew her attention to a van selling fish. Deciding it would just be the very thing for Logan Murray's dinner, she hastened to make yet another purchase. Jamie, following her eagerly, said he liked kippers, so she got a few pairs for breakfast. The man who was selling the fish asked Jamie how his father was, but seemed more interested in Thea.

He was a youngish man and she found herself subjected to several curious glances. She felt driven at last to say coolly that she was the new housekeeper at Drumlarig, which, for no reason she could think of, appeared to interest the man even more.

Fear that she might be taking too much upon herself too soon, as Logan Murray had remarked, couldn't prevent a certain feeling of satisfaction, as she drove home. She had only been at Drumlarig a day, yet it felt more like weeks. It must surely be that her roots were here, that because she had been born here she was fitting in so naturally. Logan Murray might not think so, but as she didn't like him she wouldn't let this worry her. He had a strange effect on her and she was sure they could never be friends, but Jamie she did like and, she tried to convince herself, it was because of him she must stay.

When she took Logan's dinner up, again on a nicely set tray, to her surprise he accepted it without protest. He even glanced at the tray with something approaching interest, as if it was a long time since he had had such a daintily cooked meal. Thea had baked the fish, to make it a little more appetising, and served it with a lightly buttered sauce. In a small glass dish she had put some fresh fruit salad and icecream, which she thought he might find refreshing, and lastly she had placed on the tray a jug of freshly ground, freshly made coffee, the aroma of that alone, she considered, being enough to tempt any man's appetite.

While he might have raised no protest, Logan Murray certainly wasn't going to overload her with appreciation. As she put the tray down where he could reach it he was disinclined to talk. He waved her away, saying he could manage, and she was so pleased he hadn't refused to have anything that she scarcely noticed he didn't thank her. She was even happier to notice that he took a long drink from the jug of barley water she had made, and wiping his lips with a sigh of satisfaction as she departed. It wasn't until she was through the door that she paused to wonder if his pleasure had been at her going, rather than the barley water.

Later, when she went back to collect his tray, she found him sleeping, so she quietly made up the fire, then left him. He had eaten almost all his supper and his fever appeared to have gone. She could see he was much cooler and she hoped he would sleep until morning. As she stood for a moment looking down at him, she wondered, her pulse beating unevenly, if it would be the last time she would see him asleep.

Next morning Thea woke early in the room she had been given. It was still dark and she felt confused, not instantly remembering where she was. She thought, when she first drowsily opened her eyes, that she was in London, in her flat, and she almost turned over and went to sleep again.

Almost, but not quite. With a jerk she sat up as full realisation came to her. She wasn't in her flat, she was at Drumlarig, and it must be years since she had woken with such a feeling of eagerness. Allowing herself a luxurious moment of contemplation, she puzzled over it, unable to account for it. It must be that because, until recently, her grandparents had ruled her life perhaps too strictly this sense of new-found freedom was going to her head. Thea's smooth brow creased. Freedom wasn't quite the right word. It was more the feeling of being in control, where before she had been the one to be controlled. Even when Logan Murray managed to leave his bed, which couldn't be for a while yet, if she was to be his housekeeper he couldn't seriously interfere with the way she ran the house. Or could he? Not even Grandmother had dared do that, with her housekeepers. Dismissing such a thought as foolish, Thea dreamed happily on, unprepared for the rude shock that awaited her on her arrival downstairs.

Her first change of mood came when she suddenly realised, with a gasp of dismay, that she had slept soundly all night and Logan Murray's fire might be out. As she tumbled out of bed the coldness of the room made her shiver and, when she managed to stumble over it to switch on the light, the bareness of it didn't help. There was a small makeshift bathroom attached to her bedroom, also a small sitting room. Martha had explained that it was the housekeeper's official suite. Unfortunately it was too shabbily furnished to be half as grand as Martha made it sound.

Thea hadn't felt quite so amused when Martha had gone on to say that the housekeepers at Drumlarig were expected to spend their free time, if they ever had any, either here or in the kitchen. Then Thea had recalled what Logan Murray had said about her taking the freedom of the house —until he was up and about!

Plain enough speaking! Thea shrugged as she quickly sluiced her sleepy face in cold water. No one hinted in this house. The sitting room was not very comfortable but, given time, she could probably improve it. It might, even as it was, be no worse than the huge, neglected rooms downstairs. Yesterday she had peeped in one or two of them and had not been impressed by what she had seen. Two of the downstairs rooms, she had noticed, were not even furnished. There were all the signs that they had been, but now they were quite bare and empty.

Putting on the skirt and sweater she had brought with her, Thea brushed out her hair and tied it back, so that it lay like a sleek, shining cap against her small, graceful head, guaranteed, she felt sure, to make her look older. Little did she realise it had quite the opposite effect. Then, just as she was, her grey eyes sparkling, her smooth cheeks glowing pink from the cold water, she ran downstairs. She would get the kitchen fire going before taking up more logs for Logan Murray, then get them both a nice hot cup of tea.

CHAPTER FOUR

I⊤ wasn't until she reached the kitchen that Thea felt the first stirrings of an unwelcome premonition. But not until she pushed open the door did she realise why she had gone suddenly cold as she crossed the hall. Logan Murray was sitting on the edge of the wide, scrubbed table, calmly observing the cessation of all movement in his new housekeeper's limbs.

From this distance Thea stared at him, knowing it must be stupid to be so stunned but unable to help it. Logan Murray was here, downstairs and dressed in his kilt, dominating the room. Dominating herself, too, it would appear, as she was strangely bereft of speech. He looked grey and strained, but he had about him an air of determination, an arrogance of bearing. Thea recognised, with a sinking heart, that Logan Murray up was an entirely different proposition from the man in bed, and even there he had been a man to be reckoned with.

'Good morning.' His voice, cool and clipped, was a sure indication that nothing had been missed in his education. He broke the silence, which Thea was not immediately capable of doing, in a way she envied. He didn't say she was too early or accuse her of being late, he simply acknowledged her, from his superior position, as he might have done Martha or Duncan. But for them, she was certain, there would have been more warmth.

Thea was so surprised she could only stand dumbly and stare. She took in the breadth of his shoulders under his rough woollen shirt, the strength and suppleness of his tall body without really seeing anything. He might look well in a kilt, but he had ruined all her plans. She had seen herself nursing him for several more days, until he had come to realise she was indispensable. Now here he was, ready, she suspected, to go out and tend his stock. He obviously had no intention of going back to bed and allowing her to look after him.

'Mr Murray,' she found her voice at last, 'you aren't well enough to be up! Do you think it's wise?'

'Probably not,' he agreed, 'but I don't doubt I'll survive. My animals might not, though, if they don't receive proper attention.'

'You have a shepherd. He's around.'

'I also have a housekeeper, it appears, who's already trying to run my life. You might have proved yourself useful, Miss Andrews, but I hope you know where to stop.'

While he stared at her narrowly, Thea digested this. He had mentioned her usefulness, but she doubted if he had meant it as a compliment. Probably he was just stating a fact, as he saw it. She didn't think he would waste much time praising anybody.

His green eyes, which she thought saw far too much, studied her closely—and sceptically. 'I would rather you'd been twenty years older, fifty instead of thirty, but perhaps you'll be able to work harder than a woman twice your age.'

'Yes, Mr Murray.' Feeling she was being evaluated like a piece of farm machinery, she took all her restraint to produce a meek reply. His unexpected appearance had unnerved her, while his remarks aroused her resentment, but he remained arrogantly cool, in no way disturbed.

'How about making a cup of tea?' His sardonic request breaking her reverie, startled her almost as much as his presence had done. Quickly she averted her eyes from his dark face and reached blindly for the kettle. As she filled it, she couldn't help stealing another glance at his kilt.

'Haven't you seen a man in a kilt before, Miss Andrews?'

'Of course,' she stammered, tearing his eyes away from him again, 'but never so—so close.'

'It's nothing to get alarmed about,' he replied mockingly, without taking his eyes from her.

His glance she could feel boring into her, causing a peculiar sensation, like pins and needles to run all over her skin. She swung back to him, a small flicker of desperation driving her. 'Mr Murray!'

'Yes, Miss Andrews?' he encouraged sardonically.

'Oh, nothing.' Regretting her half anxious impulse as she met the green-flecked glitter in his eyes, she sighed. 'I was merely going to repeat what I've just said, but I realise you won't listen to me. I'm sure you shouldn't be out of bed. And after all, I'm here.'

His voice was full of hard irony, extremely dry. 'Don't you think that's one good reason why I should be out of bed. I have a would-be housekeeper to interview.'

'Would-be...?'

'Yes, Miss Andrews. No need to look so surprised. I might be forced to take what I can get, for Jamie's sake, but you surely don't expect to get a job without having to answer a few questions first? And gaining, in return, a little information yourself?'

'Information?' Pouring boiling water in the teapot, Thea was scarcely aware of what she was doing.

'Regarding wages, etc. Free time, what your duties are to be.' He paused, his eyes roving contemplatively over her, a slight frown creasing his forehead. 'Haven't you ever been employed before, girl?'

'Er—yes.' She almost said no. Her lips had actually formed the first letter which she had swallowed hastily, but she could see his suspicion was aroused.

'I think you'd better get yourself sorted out before ten, Miss Andrews, which is when I will see you. If nothing keeps me outside, I'll be in the library, or what was once the library, down the hall.'

Nodding a reluctant agreement, Thea poured the hot tea, then asked what time he took breakfast.

'About eight.' He was still staring at her and she wished he would look elsewhere. It wasn't as if there was any kindness in his eyes, and his steady regard confused her.

'Am I to take Jamie to school this morning?' she asked, as he finished his tea and reached for the shabby tweed jacket which she noticed he had laid on the table beside him.

'Would you?' For a moment he looked relieved, as though he had found the task of regularly ferrying a small boy to school irksome.

'I enjoy driving—and I promise to take care,' she added, again wondering at her strange desire to reassure him. She was even more surprised at herself when he merely nodded and went out, without a single word of thanks.

By eight she had porridge made and ready to serve, kippers under the grill and a pile of toast waiting to go into the toaster. But only half of her mind was on breakfast, the other half was with Logan, anxious about what he was doing. He didn't appear to realise he was still ill, and she knew instinctively he was. The morning was dark, she could hear the rain. What if he had collapsed, was lying helpless somewhere with no one to help him?

She was just about to go and search for him, without regard for his possible annoyance, when he came in, followed by old Martha. Jamie was already tucking in and she suddenly remembered she hadn't asked Logan where he usually took his breakfast. She had set him a place here without thinking, and she hated to think that she had risked his displeasure yet again.

Her feelings were mixed when he assured her that the kitchen did well enough. 'I've long since given up being a gentleman,' he replied dryly. 'I only use the dining-room when I have guests.'

'Wouldn't you like your dinner served there?' She wasn't sure why she pursued the subject. 'I mean, there's Jamie ...'

As she slowed to an uncertain halt, he smiled without humour. 'You mean I should be setting him an example? Is this what you're trying tactfully to say, Miss Andrews?'

'Well, as he doesn't have anyone else!' she exclaimed, then stopped abruptly, as his eyes narrowed.

'So,' he said with deceptive softness, looking around the table, 'someone's been busy?'

'I told her,' Martha confessed unrepentantly, from her stool near the fire, where Thea was to learn she always sat until Logan had finished his meal. 'She asked and I told her.'

'Oh, please ...' Thea found her face going scarlet with guilt as she stared at them all, 'I didn't mean to pry or seem curious ...'

'But you were about the master's wife,' Martha cut in craftily, 'and you'd liked to have known a lot more than ...'

'Enough!' Logan snapped, his patience reaching its limits. 'I'll see you later, Miss Andrews. If you have anything more to ask, then kindly ask me.'

Thea moved towards the cooker, not realising what she was doing. When he spoke like that he shook her profoundly, no use pretending he didn't. Whenever he looked at her the strangest sensations came over her, sensations as sweet as they were savage. She would have the chance, when he saw her at ten, to refuse the job she had hoped he was going to offer. Much better to take the opportunity and go. To go before she got in any deeper!

His health and temper might not be good this morning, but there seemed little wrong with his appetite. She noticed, as he accepted a plate of kippers, grilled to perfection, that he had finished all his porridge. As she carefully sugared a huge cup of hot, strong tea before placing it before him, she frowned. He was right, of course; she shouldn't have mentioned his wife to anyone, but he could have made allowances for her, as a stranger. And she hadn't really asked out of idle curiosity. It had been prompted more from concern. As she passed him hot toast and marmalade, her eyes met his, her own full of unconscious pleading, but she found nothing even remotely encouraging in his black, shuttered stare.

At ten she went, as he had instructed, to the library. In her hands she carried two mugs of coffee. She had meant to set a tray, but had been so busy there hadn't been time. It wasn't that she particularly wanted any coffee herself, but it might be something to look at, and to do with her hands during the forthcoming interview.

Logan was already there, standing with his back to the empty hearth. Thea wished she had thought of lighting a fire. Without one the room was cold and sombre in appearance. There were two easy chairs, but the bookshelves which lined the walls were almost empty, while the carpets and curtains were quite threadbare.

Putting down the mugs she carried on a low table, Thea glanced slowly around. Why, when her mother had given the impression that the Murrays of Drumlarig were fairly affluent, was Logan Murray living like a man without a penny to his name? There seemed only one answer, that Logan's wife had spent all his money. Perhaps this was why he was being so careful now. It was a shame, though, that Jamie had to be the one to suffer.

The slight shiver she gave was misconstrued. 'Are you cold, Miss Andrews?'

'Not really,' she shook her fair head, 'but wouldn't you like a fire?'

'No, I would not. Maybe when the weather gets colder.'

'Colder?'

A smile, with its usual hint of cynicism, curled his hard lips, 'I can see you're full of Southern softness, Miss Andrews, but if you are to live here then you must be prepared to put up with somewhat harsher conditions. You live in London, I suppose?'

'Yes.'

He took the coffee she passed him, then put it down again, while she wrapped her fingers around her own mug in an effort to keep her hands warm. 'Your family? Do they know where you are? I realise you're quite old enough to be accountable to no one, but I should appreciate a few particulars.'

'I have no parents,' she said slowly, 'nor any other relations. My father died before I was born.'

His dark brows rose. 'So you're quite a free agent. What made you leave London?'

'I—I think I was feeling restless and decided to have a look at Scotland.'

'You didn't choose a good time of year.'

'Perhaps not, but I hadn't anything else to do, Mr Murray.'

The quick tightening of his mouth warned her that he wouldn't tolerate her indifferent tone. 'There seems little point in another review of the way you arrived here, but have you ever done domestic work before?'

His sceptical glance, resting on her slim, pale hands, told her why he felt doubtful about this. 'Yes,' she said, setting her rounded chin stubbornly.

'Where did you learn to cook the way you do?'

'Cook?' She met the dark intentness of his gaze hesitantly. 'I have no professional qualifications, if that's what you're after. I suppose I just picked it up.' Gran had employed a cook where they had lived in the country and, because Thea always had to be doing something, she had often watched her to pass the time. Mabel had occasionally allowed her to try her hand at a few dishes and pronounced her a born cook. When they had come to London, where the household had been suddenly smaller, and Gran ill, she had done most of the cooking while the housekeeper had done the nursing.

Somehow her answer appeared to satisfy Logan, as if it was one he could understand. 'If I employ you,' he said abruptly, 'I will expect you to work hard for very little,' he named a sum which almost made her gasp. As he heard it, his brows rose sardonically. 'Do you still wish to stay?'

'I don't care what you pay me,' she retorted, much, she suspected, to his surprise. Had he hoped to drive her away by offering an insult of a wage? 'And,' she added anxiously, 'I don't care what I have to do, just as long as I can stay a while.'

He came closer, until he could stare down into her face, so that he might judge without mistake her exact reactions to his next query. 'It seems you're after some kind of sanctuary, Miss Andrews. Are you hiding from a man?'

Silently Thea cursed the guilty flush which spread over her face. 'No,' she stammered, then thinking of Jerry, though not, she was sure, in the same way Logan meant, she finished helplessly, 'Not really.'

'So,' Logan's eyes remained fixed on her face, a trace of harsh violence lurking somewhere in their green depth, 'there is someone! Well, I warn you, Miss Andrews, I'll have no camp-followers here. Or any man you might pick up in the locality. You're attractive enough, with your childish face and provocative figure, but whatever you do in that direction, you will do elsewhere.'

'Mr Murray!' Rage sparkled in Thea's grey eyes, turning them into twin clouds with a storm behind them. Just about to tell him he could keep his worthless job, she remembered she did need a sanctuary. She thought, too, of all that his family had done for her mother; how her mother had often longed for the means to repay them, a means which her in-laws, Thea's grandparents, had always denied her. How could she walk out on Logan Murray and his son when they were so obviously in need of someone? And where would she go? Back to London, to her old way of life, which was somehow becoming, with every hour, less and less inviting.

'Mr Murray,' she began again, this time quietly, 'you

don't have to worry about anything like that. I have no particular boy-friend in London, nor do I intend looking for one here.'

He still considered her closely and she couldn't read what was at the back of his enigmatical eyes. For a moment she thought the talk of boy-friends, with its implied implications, had stirred him. Yet if it had made him think momentarily of sex, she couldn't believe he was associating it with her. There must be enough women who would be only too willing to give a man as handsome as Logan Murray everything he demanded. Remembering the effect of his unconscious mouth, Thea trembled. She must take great care not to become one of them!

'Right!' She jumped as his crisp voice cut through her uneasy thoughts. Before she could speak, he began swiftly outlining her duties, acquainting her of several more rules and regulations until she feared she would never remember the half of them. Then he paused, but when she supposed thankfully that he had finished, he shot at her, 'I understand you went shopping yesterday?'

'Yes.' She could see nothing wrong with that. 'We were short of so many things, but I paid for everything and kept the bills. To show you, of course.'

'How much?' he demanded grimly, with no regard for her conciliatory little ending.

She told him.

'Let me have the accounts and I'll settle with you. In future bear in mind that that's almost the sum I allow for an entire week.'

'A week?' Why, she had spent more on herself!

'Yes, a week!' he repeated, making sure, she was certain, that she understood.

'But ...' she began, her eyes completely betraying her incredulous thoughts.

'Miss Andrews!' this time his glance was laced with green flames, 'I will not have you coming here dictating to

me. Didn't I warn you, you'd have to rid yourself of that
idea, once I was out of bed. Well, I'm out of bed now, so
listen carefully. You aren't my idea of a housekeeper and
never will be. Unfortunately, as I keep on learning, beg-
gars can't be choosers. However, that's not to say I'll put
up with anything. Either you obey me and do as I say—or
out! And there'll be no ifs or buts about it. You will be
back on the road so fast, not even your shadow will be
able to keep up with you.'

Furious though Thea felt at this less than gentle lecture,
she could see no immediate way of actively opposing
the man. The warning he had given was too clear, and she
guessed he wouldn't think twice before carrying out his
threats, some part of her being well aware that he was
already regretting having allowed her to stay in the first
place. She wasn't even sure that she dared protest again
about the money he expected her to manage on. It seemed
a terribly small amount on which to feed a family, unless
they were prepared to live on turnips! There were plenty
of those in the pit outside. Back in the kitchen, on a
piece of paper at the kitchen table, she wrote out a menu.
Turnips—Fried—grilled—boiled—baked. Turnip fritters
with sugar, Steamed turnip pudding with custard . . .

When Martha asked what she was doing, she screwed up
the piece of paper and threw it crossly away, without replying. Unfortunately Jamie found it before dinner and
showed it to his father, giggling as though he had found a
comic strip of jokes. Thea's cheeks flamed as she met
Logan Murray's cold eyes. He knew what it was about, if
Jamie didn't, and he was not so amused as his son.

Convinced she had blotted her copybook good and
proper, Thea spent the next few days going through the
house like a small fury. Industriously she brushed and
polished, finding so much dust that she couldn't help
wondering what Logan's previous housekeepers had been
doing. What she was trying to prove by such a burst of

energy she wasn't sure, and when Logan eventually asked her this sharply, she didn't know what to say.

'I think it's your first taste of being told what to do, or possibly what you can't do, and you don't like it,' he said coolly when he caught her laying a fire in the library. With an equally cool interest he studied the smut of soot on her delicate little nose before dropping to the soft curves of the mobile mouth below it. 'You daren't, for some reason I'm not yet aware of, go against my authority, so you're trying to get at me through the house, or rather the state of it.'

'No, I'm not,' she denied, flinging back the fine gold hair which kept getting in her eyes, hating to admit he could be right. Gran and Grandfather had always ruled her life, but within the limits they had set she had been able to do much as she liked. Taking a deep breath, she avoided his searching gaze. 'I'm just trying to make the place more comfortable, for Jamie's sake. You can't sit in the kitchen, now that I'm here, but with a little effort this room could be made nice.'

'Why can't I sit in the kitchen now you're here?' he countered idly.

'Didn't your other housekeepers mind?' She frowned, wishing he wouldn't challenge her every statement.

He laughed. 'I rarely have time to sit, you silly girl, and when I do it's usually in here. I do all my office work in the evenings.'

'But when your wife was alive——' she began, then stopped, just as suddenly, as his face darkened.

'My wife never lived here,' he enlightened Thea curtly, 'so you don't have to speculate about that.'

Thea knew some things were better left alone, but a kind of reckless indiscretion lay over her. 'Then, if she was never here, how could Martha not like her?'

'Martha did see her once or twice,' he agreed.

'Then . . .'

'Miss Andrews!' Logan took her arm, looking as if he could cheerfully break it, just to enjoy her cry of pain. Roughly he jerked her to her feet, from her crouching position beside the fireplace. So near, she could see the grim set of his strong mouth, the thick, spiky lashes which framed the brilliant green of his eyes. 'Miss Andrews,' he turned her harshly towards the door, 'will you kindly go and leave me in peace! Isn't it time, anyway, that you went to fetch Jamie?'

'Jamie?' She was trembling as he let go of her, for both his tone and touch had been vicious. She had forgotten about Jamie, and he worried if she wasn't on time. 'Yes,' she wrenched her eyes from the hard face above her, 'I'll go now, once I've washed my hands. I—I'm sorry if I've upset you.'

He shook his head, but she didn't think it was to indicate that what she said didn't matter. It was more as though he was attempting to shake away the past, which had returned unbidden because of her foolish remarks.

She couldn't find the keys for the Land Rover. They seemed to have disappeared from their usual hook on the kitchen dresser. Neither were they in her jeans pockets, nor in the pockets of her coat. Eventually Martha, awakening from one of her many small naps, informed her that Himself had taken them earlier and that she would likely find them left in the vehicle!

They were, and muttering uncomplimentary things under her breath, Thea raced all the way to the village. For all she positively risked her neck, on reaching the village school she found Jamie had gone. One of the other pupils, who was still hanging around, said Jamie had taken the short cut home over the moors.

Feeling full of remorse because he must have thought she wasn't coming, Thea raced back to Drumlarig. Already it was growing dark, and Martha had once mentioned that when Jamie came home across the moors at night he often stopped to play by the loch, something his father had forbidden. The last time he had done it, he had been sent to bed without his supper.

Knowing how hungry Jamie always was by dinner time, Thea thought this cruel, and was determined he shouldn't be sent to bed without his dinner tonight. Not when it hadn't been his fault that she had been late and missed him at school. He ought to have known she would turn up, but at his age it was very easy to panic. She should have watched the time and not let Murray provoke her.

Parking the Land Rover, she didn't go back into the house but set off immediately along the moorland track to meet him. With any luck they would soon be home and Murray need never know what had happened. Anxiously she realised that her growing friendship with Jamie might as yet be too delicate to survive the grim onslaught of his father's temper.

About a mile from the house, on the path which clung to the edge of a wide stretch of water to the north of it, in the distance she saw Jamie coming. Torn with anxiety that something might have happened to him, she felt relief surge through her as she caught sight of his small figure. Almost desperately she waved her arms and began to run. When she came to where a tumbling stream ran deeply into the loch, she didn't stop but plunged recklessly through it.

She was very wet when she dragged herself clumsily out on the other side, but this didn't seem to matter. What with the rain and the rivers, she didn't seem to have been dry since she came here! It was Jamie. Thea was so pleased to see him, she simply flung her arms around him with a gasp of relief. Whether he appreciated this or not, she wasn't sure, but at least he didn't immediately move away.

'Jamie!' she choked breathlessly. 'Oh, Jamie, I'm sorry I was late coming to fetch you. I thought you were sure to be lost.'

'I never get lost,' he said reproachfully, but to her surprise he did hug her quickly back and she fancied his lips trembled. It was obviously a long time since anyone had shown him affection like this.

Then he was all grown up again. Pushing himself out of her arms, he scowled as he touched her damp cheek. 'You're wet, Thea. We'd better get home.'

Home sounded suddenly so good that she laughed, her vivacious young face lighting up. 'I'm getting used to being wet, Jamie. You haven't exactly the driest of climates in Scotland.'

'Perhaps not,' he sounded just like his father, 'but you look as though you've been in the burn.' Casually he retained her hand, as if to make sure she didn't fall in again.

'Well, there's no bridge.'

'There is one, about twenty yards further up the river. The loch often overflows, so it would be no good putting a bridge right on the side of it, would it? Didn't you see it?'

Feeling distinctly foolish, Thea muttered something about not having had time to look. She did feel better when they came to the bridge and she found it consisted of only three narrow planks, which, as a stranger, she felt she might be excused for missing. 'I'll know the next time,' she smiled ruefully, trying to hide from Jamie how cold and uncomfortable she was from her soaking.

Having hoped to avoid Logan, she despaired on finding him waiting for them, having apparently drawn his own conclusions from the crazily parked Land Rover as to what had happened.

He appeared startled, however, when he saw Thea's bedraggled state. 'What on earth have you been up to this time?' he snapped, ignoring his son.

Thea, because she was cold and rather miserable, snapped back, 'Is it my fault that you don't build your bridges in the right places?'

'Thea fell in the river and she was mad,' Jamie giggled.

'She hugged me and I got wet, too. You should have seen her!'

Logan cast him a sharp glance. 'That's enough from you, young man. Miss Andrews should remember she's a house-keeper, not a court jester.'

So he hadn't forgotten her joke about the turnips? In a gesture of unconscious defiance she tossed her head. Un-fortunately her hair was still damp and she only succeeded in showering the floor with drops of water.

Extreme exasperation made a grim line of Logan's mouth. 'For heaven's sake, girl, were you completely sub-merged in the—er—river?'

'I fell.' She was quite aware he had moderated his lan-guage for Jamie's sake, not hers.

'Then you'd better go and change right away,' he ad-vised, without a trace of sympathy. 'One bout of sickness in the house is all we can afford, for the time being.'

It must have been because of the successive soakings she had endured that all the next day Thea felt hot and feverish. She had an awful suspicion that she had been overtaken by one of the sudden severe colds that she had been sus-ceptible to as a child. By the time dinner was over and Jamie had gone to bed, she was feeling quite ill. To her dismay, her legs gave out under her and she slumped in a chair by the kitchen table, wondering how she was to get upstairs.

Logan had gone out with a lantern to see to a cow which was calving. Thea hoped when he returned he would go straight to the library. It worried her when he didn't. Coming into the kitchen, he removed his coat before sitting down to take off his heavy rubber boots. The sight of his dark head, as he bent to undo the laces, affected her oddly, forcing her to look away.

Not being able to find the energy to ask about the young animal he was tending, and which they all felt anxious about, she stared down at her hands lying on the table, wondering why they were so tightly clenched. Murray still didn't look completely well, but this didn't seem to hide his vitality which must be a natural and unconquerable part of him. Something dynamic about him seemed to reach out ruthlessly and touch her. It was a feeling which had begun on the evening he kissed her and had grown rapidly ever since, in spite of her efforts to fight it. It wasn't sensible, but then she didn't suppose anything about her coming here was.

'Are you all right?'

Because her nerves were on edge, Logan's blunt query made her jump. Deciding hastily that a little truth might be more convincing than assuring him she was, she looked away from his suspicious stare. 'Just a headache.'

'You're croaking!'

In slight desperation, her voice rose. 'It's nothing. I'll be fine—if you'd just leave me alone.'

'You don't look it.' He took no notice of her pleading, his voice silky. 'I like to look after my employees, you know.'

'Don't worry,' she was stung to retort, 'if I can't work I won't claim any wages.'

The silence which followed this outburst was so taut it compelled her to look at him. As quickly she averted her eyes from the cold grimness of his. Did he have to be so domineering, and angry with it? Surely he didn't expect her to take everything he threw at her lying down! All the same, she wished she had something of his strength and height. Beside him she felt absolutely helpless.

In an attempt to convince him she was near normal, she kept her hot, flushed face turned from him and said quietly, 'If the calf hasn't arrived yet you'll probably be staying up until it does.'

'Probably.'

She tried again. 'I'll make you something to drink and a sandwich, then I think I'll go to bed.'

'Go to bed now, Miss Andrews, and I'll bring you something up with something in it.'

'No!' She had to protest against such calculating authority, and stood up too quickly. Immediately the room began to spin and it was her own distressed cry she heard as Logan caught her in his arms.

Muttering something about women and their natural stupidity, he strode upstairs with Thea clinging helplessly to his neck, uncaring for the moment what he thought of her. It must be crazy to think, with her head going around and her stomach churning, that for the first time in her life she felt completely secure.

Upstairs, he laid her gently on her bed where she lay shivering. He watched the tremors going through her slender body with a frown on his face. 'This room's too cold,' he exclaimed curtly. 'I'll light a fire.'

'You're beginning to sound like me!' She tried to laugh lightly, but it didn't sound right. Her voice was hoarse, deepening his frown.

He lifted a rug, placing it over her. 'Lie still,' he commanded, 'while I get you something. You need heat, both inside and out.'

Soon he was back, holding her firmly, making her sip from a glass of brandy. Her own hands shook when she tried to hold the glass herself and she felt grateful when he held it for her.

He had a fire going in no time at all, working with an efficiency which might have surprised her if she had been fully conscious of what he was doing. The brandy and hot tea he brought had appeared to do her good at first, but now she began feeling worse. Spasms started shaking her, bringing a fine perspiration to her brow, a cold, clammy sensation to the rest of her body.

'I feel sick, Logan,' she cried wildly.

He had gone out to wash his hands, but her sharp, panic-stricken cry brought him quickly to the side of her bed. His face was momentarily startled, as though her strangled words woke memories long forgotten. 'You sound like a child I once knew,' he said, reaching down for her. 'It's a comfort to know you definitely aren't a child, I'm beginning to think,' he finished enigmatically, as he carried her to the bathroom.

Here he held her while she was violently ill, talking to her softly, his hand on her head, calming and soothing her when she began to weep. When it was over she managed to rinse her mouth with warm water, but it was Logan who gently washed her face before lifting her in his arms again to carry her back to bed.

Vaguely she was aware that her sweater and skirt were damp and stained, but she was still too dizzy to do anything about them. She was only dimly aware of Logan undressing her, although she tried to protest as her sweater came over her head, as she remembered that underneath it she wore only scrappy bits of satin and lace, scarcely worthy of the name they bore.

'Please, Logan,' she whispered, her hands going out blindly to deter his, 'I'm sure I can manage.'

Forcing herself to look at him, she found nothing in the impersonal green of his eyes to alarm her. Yet she felt her pulse jerk wildly in her throat as he looked at her.

Grimly he retorted, 'I think the time for false modesy is past, Thea. You're ill and you need help and that's all there is to it. I assure you there's nothing at all for you to worry about. I'm not sure where all this is leading to, but whatever happens, trust me to be able to handle it.'

CHAPTER FIVE

But could he? Thea didn't think anyone could handle the primitive feelings of fever and emotion which suddenly raged through her. Yet, as he began covering her carefully with her bedclothes, she fought for control with a formal remark.

'It's very good of you to bother,' she didn't look at the dark face bending over her as she spoke, 'but I don't think you should be here.'

As his hands tucked the sheet firmly around her she shivered as it tightened abruptly. 'Perhaps not,' he replied dryly, 'but I believe I said more or less the same thing to you in my room, when you helped me.'

'This is different,' she protested weakly. 'I'm only your housekeeper. You're not supposed to be looking after me—not this way.'

His expression altered slightly, as if he realised this but had a mind of his own. 'Things seldom stand still, Thea. Our relationship seems to have been far from ordinary from the beginning. Some facts you have to face and learn to accept. You're a grown woman and you've been around. You must know men find you attractive. As for myself, I always have a strange feeling that we've met somewhere before. Maybe,' he added, 'in another life.'

Watching his indifferent shrug with dazed eyes, she tried to hang on to her fast failing sense of humour. 'Maybe I was your slave, even then? Centuries ago I might not have been called a housekeeper.'

'Perhaps not.' To her astonishment, he flicked her hot cheek with a soft brush of his fingers. 'Now try and get some sleep. You're in no condition to start solving those kind of mysteries.'

His touch had soothed, as he might have intended it should, for her heavy eyes closed and she surrendered to the darkness which invaded her exhausted body. She felt safe with Logan beside her, and convinced he wouldn't go away.

Some time later she woke to find him sitting reading by her bed. It wasn't, she thought, an agricultural paper, but she couldn't really see. When she struggled to sit up, an unconscious urgency upon her to prove she was better, he jumped to his feet and immediately pushed her back against her pillows.

'Stop it, Thea!' His hands were as firm as his voice as he settled on the edge of the bed to hold her still, 'Stop struggling, there's a good girl, and you'll soon be all right.'

He must think she was delirious, as he had been himself. Recalling how hot she had been when she had fallen asleep, she thought this not improbable. 'Have I been rambling?' she asked breathlessly, doing as she was told but beseeching him with huge anxious eyes. 'I used to sometimes, when I had a cold as a child.'

Taking her wrist, he frowned at the quickening pulse. 'I thought you still were,' he confessed, with a sigh. 'You've been very restless, I was afraid to leave you for long. But don't worry, you haven't given any secrets away.'

'What time is it?' she asked weakly, clinging to his hand.

'Just after twelve.'

'You ought to be in bed.'

He smiled slightly. 'Twelve o'clock isn't always my bed-time, and you haven't had my undivided attention, you know. You might be happy to hear that Jamie's pet cow has been blessed with a rather good-looking son.'

Sudden unpredictable tears stung Thea's eyelids and overflowed. 'Oh, yes! And won't Jamie be delighted, too? He has so little.'

Even as she spoke, she stiffened, blessing her too-hasty tongue. Why must she deliberately arouse Logan's anger

with her tactlessness? It surprised her that he wasn't unduly disturbed.

'Jamie might have a lot more than appearances suggest,'
he paused enigmatically, without taking his eyes from her.
'If you, my little hothead, would spare a moment to think
about it some time, you might see this. However, there
could be some changes in the near future which might
benefit him. I'll admit a man doesn't always make a good
job of rearing a child alone.'

What did Murray mean by that? Aware of a crushing
heaviness of spirit, Thea couldn't bring herself to ask him.
Now that she was living here she didn't want to think
about changes. Confused, she whispered, 'Well, anyway,
it was nice of you to look after me. I do feel better—my
fevers never last long.'

'Don't they?'

'No.' To convince him, she sat up again too quickly and
found her head swimming. As the dizziness caught her
she fell forward with a gasp of alarm, straight into his
arms. Swiftly they were there to support her and she
clutched helplessly at the hard muscles of his chest.

'You try too hard!' He sounded faintly impatient, yet his
arms tightened slightly and he didn't immediately let her
go.

Thea didn't know why she just wanted to cling to him,
to have the feeling of his arms around her, holding her com-
fortingly close. He would do the same for Jamie or one of
his dogs. She wasn't asking for any special attention, just
enough to alleviate the crushing sense of aloneness which
sometimes came over her.

'Logan,' she breathed, momentarily forgetting the bar-
riers between them, 'would you kiss me?'

As she raised her mouth, in what she feared afterwards
must have been a wanton invitation, he hesitated, staring
down at her. She had forgotten how little she had on, that
she lay, semi-naked, in his arms. All she was conscious of

was an urgent need for closer contact, to establish something which might make her forget the changes he had referred to. An underlying necessity to discover if the feelings he had previously aroused, when he had kissed her, were real was something she was barely aware of.

'I suppose I could,' he murmured thickly, his eyes on the tender curves of her mouth. 'At your age you must know what you're doing.'

Only half hearing his remark, she nodded her head, the quickening beat of her heart seeming to make her deaf to everything else.

Yet, as he bent down to her, she wasn't prepared for the total possession of his kiss when it came, nor the years of experience behind it, which mocked her first bewildered attempts to match it. Startled, she tried to draw back, but his arms slid completely around her, crushing her slender body closer, while one hand grasped a handful of her silky hair, pulling her head back to take the full force of his hard mouth.

The hardness of his chest made her breasts ache. She had invited his lovemaking, but it was more than she had bargained for. His mouth was like an assault. As the kiss hardened and lengthened she couldn't move. All the sensation which she had thought she must have imagined, in his bedroom, was there. It flooded her body, jerking her convulsively against him, bringing a sharp fear which tensed her slight limbs virginally against the instant hardening of his, as the same excitement mounted sensuously within her.

The drowning sensation was too real to be bearable. Frantically, as he groaned against her, her hands clutched his arms, as though in a desperate attempt to save herself. This was not as she had planned. If she had been guilty of planning anything at all, it had only been one chaste little kiss. Nothing like this. Not something that was turning her limbs to jelly and threatened to render her completely helpless.

As the pressure of his mouth increased roughly, her lungs ached with the effort of trying to breathe, and if she had almost forgotten what she was doing so, apparently, had Logan. His arms tightened with an urgent passion that seemed to penetrate every pore of her being.

The feeling was so sweeping that she subconsciously fought against it by clenching her lips tightly. She found the strength to do this even while her head was swimming. Vaguely, she fancied she was doing rather well until, as though he was aware of her resistance and seeking to punish her for it, his hands moved around to caress the rosy peaks of her breasts. It was then she was lost, as with an involuntary gasp her lips parted under his.

Moments later the wild panic returned, as she became aware of rising emotions which she couldn't control. Logan must have known what she was trying to fight, but he didn't seem noticeably intent on helping her. Instinct warned her that something might be pushing him harder than she knew. A certain passionate hunger was conveying itself in the hot, sweet exploration of his mouth, his momentary blindness to everything but his own deep needs. Unwittingly perhaps, she had put a match to something explosive. If she got hurt she could only blame herself, for hadn't she invited—begged him and tempted?

'Let me go!' she gasped, with superhuman effort dragging her bruised mouth away from his.

He refused thickly, 'It's not enough, Thea, not nearly enough!'

Raising heavy, distracted eyes, she saw the flush of colour over his cheekbones, his green eyes darkening to near black. He wasn't angry—she realised weakly that his strongest emotion at the moment wasn't anger but desire. In a kind of mute protest she shook her fair head, but she hadn't the strength left to fight him.

From her manner of conveying it, Logan obviously read her protest as a form of agreement. Gently he smoothed the heavy hair away from her damp forehead, as though to give her breathing space, and his hands caressed the long line of her throat, pausing on the pulse that beat there frantically. His touch was insistent but kind and she couldn't resist it. With a trembling sigh of pleasure, the fight went out of her as she felt his lips on her temple before he pressed them on her closed eyelids, the side of her cheek, along her jawline. Then he was covering her mouth again with deep, drugging kisses which made her only want to cry out and cling to him.

Easing away from her for a moment, he unbuttoned his shirt. Slowly he took her hands, sliding them inside it, around him, until once more she was crushed against him. Swiftly he undid the fastening on the back of her bra. From there his hands explored the slight indentation of her spine, as far as it went, before coming back to curve forcibly over her slim hips, her yielding breasts.

That she was suddenly weak and shivering didn't arouse his compassion. When his mouth again took her own, she was floating mindlessly in empty space, torn strangely by fierce flashes of blinding light. As she clung to him her fingers tightened over the hard muscles of his broad shoulders before burying themselves in the dark thickness of his hair. Helplessly she shuddered against him, gasping his name.

When she had asked him to kiss her, it had been on a quickly regretted, fever-born impulse. Never had she dreamed it would be like this. She should put a stop to it, if only because she had begun it. Logan was only taking what he thought she had offered. Ashamed, she realised that, while she wanted to go on and on, such complete devastation could only end one way. Yet many girls committed themselves easily. Why shouldn't she?

It was Logan who called a halt. He eased away from her

quite deliberately as if, Thea thought resentfully, he had a switch he could flick on and off. Her mind was dazed, but that didn't prevent this peculiar indignation coming through. She heard the harsh rasp of his breathing, felt the sweat running down his heated shoulder blades between her hands, yet his willpower was such he could turn away. It was as if he had suddenly remembered who he was and what he was doing, and was in no way pleased by the picture he saw.

He turned his head away and, as she forced herself to look at him, she could see only the taut line of his jaw. When he turned back to her his face had resumed its habitual harshness. Fascinated by his obvious ability to switch quickly from passion to indifference, she lay quite still, watching him. Grimly he removed his arms from about her and got up from off the bed. She tried to keep on looking at him, but as he began buttoning his shirt colour flared in her cheeks and her eyes fell away.

Making no attempt to touch her again, he stood staring down at her. 'You're still ill,' he said curtly, lifting a blanket and flinging it over her, something she had been too frozen to do herself. 'When you asked me to kiss you, you were probably delirious, out of your mind.'

If he was giving her an opening she had no choice but to take it. She could sense the anger in him and knew he would have no compunction about firing her. The desolation inside her grew and wept but would not be denied one bitter protest.

'Were you trying to prove I was or I wasn't?'

No way was he going to rise to the bait. 'I set out to calm you down, but it wasn't a great success.'

Only a cad would have hinted at her over-zealous response. 'Can you wonder? Going about it the way you did!'

'You weren't exactly a passive participant.'

His eyes were beginning to smoulder and she guessed he wasn't quite as cool as he liked to make out. But there would be no getting through his cool control. Never in a thousand years would a girl such as herself be able to do that.

'Thea,' he bent, putting a hand on her slumped shoulder, forcing her to meet his wary eyes. 'I don't know how much experience you've had, but I suspect not much.'

'Why should you think that?' She was crazy to go on baiting him, but she couldn't seem to help it. Caution was overlaid with a fine recklessness.

For a moment his hand tightened cruelly and his eyes glittered. 'Were you trying so very hard to please me? I think I had to persuade you every inch of the way. I'll admit, once you forgot your strange little inhibitions, you didn't hold much back, but, believe me, it's a housekeeper I want, not a mistress.'

Between clenched teeth, Thea cried tersely, 'That's the last thing I'd be!'

'Very commendable,' he sneered, 'unless your ambitions go beyond that? You wouldn't be the first who's tried and failed.'

'You're insufferable!' she gasped. 'Full of conceit! I know I asked you to kiss me, but it—it was just so I could satisfy myself about something.'

'What?' He pounced so sharply, Thea instantly regretted referring even remotely to what had happened the first night she had been at Drumlarig.

'It was nothing,' she muttered, turning suddenly to bury her throbbing head in her pillows. 'Now will you please go away!'

'With pleasure,' Logan ground out, dropping the subject, which she had feared he might pursue, and leaving the room with an ominous thud of the door.

Quietly despising herself, Thea cried herself to sleep.

When Logan came into the kitchen next morning he glanced at her pale cheeks and sighed. 'I hope you're feeling better, Miss Andrews?'

Thea was surprised to find she was. She had feared she wouldn't be able to get up, but within five minutes, after struggling out of bed, she had discovered that the worst of her cold was gone. A quick wash had alleviated any lingering symptoms and a cup of tea appeared to have completed the cure. Her head still felt heavy, her throat a little sore, but that was all.

Tilting her chin, in a way not befitting her supposed age, she said coolly, 'I'm quite recovered from everything, Mr Murray. You have no need to worry that I'll prove a nuisance.'

'I'm pleased to hear it.' His tone was as formal as her own, conveying cold satisfaction that she was being sensible. His eyes swept over her, the too tight tee-shirt, the even tighter jeans, but he said nothing about them.

Yet, as his eyes came back to the pronounced swell of her figure, a hot flush of embarrassment flooded her face and she could cheerfully have killed him. He told her, if without actually putting it into words, he wanted nothing more to do with her, while his glance said something else again. He must have a sadistic streak in him, she thought, to taunt her so deliberately. As soon as she could get to Fort William she would get something to wear more in keeping with the sedate image of a housekeeper. Until then he would just have to put up with her the way she was and stop complaining!

But she was more annoyed with herself, a few seconds later, to find she was watching him as closely, as he removed his jacket and rolled up his sleeves, revealing strongly muscled arms as he washed his hands at the sink prior to having his breakfast. His powerful figure as he stood, legs braced, did things to her heart which weren't comfortable. She could feel her breath quicken, her pulses race.

It seemed the final humiliation when he turned quickly and caught her staring at him and, though she swiftly lowered her tell-tale eyes, she was despairingly aware of what he must have read in them. That wasn't so bad, however, as being unable to hide the consternation on her face when she returned from taking Jamie to school and found Logan making arrangements to take the doctor's daughter out to dinner.

It couldn't have been a coincidence. He must have timed it to the exact minute that Thea entered the hall. He was telling Miss Stewart what time he would pick her up. 'Six-thirty sharp, which should give us plenty of time to talk before dinner.'

What did he want to talk about? Thea felt her face go white as she tried to break the fixed contact of his green eyes. With them he held her as surely as he might have with ropes around her, the mockery in them hurting her as surely as a whip. With an effort she looked away.

Jealousy, which Thea refused to admit, slowed her footsteps as she unashamedly strained to hear what else he had to say to Miss Stewart. He probably took Irene Stewart out regularly, but she didn't think Logan Murray was a man to publicise his movements. Then suddenly Thea realised his motives. This was his way of letting her know that never would a Murray of Drumlarig stoop so low as to seriously consider one of his servants attractive. Anything which had happened in an indiscreet moment had better be forgotten—or out she could go!

Like an act of dumb defiance, Thea banged the kitchen door, but Logan didn't come near. He went out the other way and Thea told herself she was glad. She had come to Drumlarig seeking peace of mind, but this was the last thing she was finding. Neither Colin nor any other of her men friends had disturbed her as much as Logan Murray—and this after only two weeks!

No sooner had Logan gone than a stranger walked in—a woman, in her early thirties, and very attractive. Need all the women who came here be so beautiful? Thea wondered despondently as, coming out of the kitchen again, she found this lady crossing the hall.

On seeing Thea, the woman stopped short. 'Oh, I'm sorry,' her brown eyes, which matched her hair, widened in bewilderment, 'I didn't know Logan had a visitor.'

'I'm not.' Thea paused, meeting the unusual dark eyes. 'I'm Thea Andrews, Mr Murray's new housekeeper.'

'You're what? Good heavens, not another!' Coming closer, she stared at Thea insolently. 'Wherever did he find you?'

Thea tried to speak evenly. 'He didn't. I saw his advert and applied.' Which was nearer the truth.

'And, as always, he's so relieved to get anyone that he never stops to have a good look at what he's getting.'

Trying to keep a grip on her temper, Thea asked politely, 'Have you called to see Mr Murray? If you have then I'm afraid you've just missed him. He's gone out.'

'I'll find him, when I'm ready.' Negligently, as though she owned the place, the woman strolled over to a chest against the wall, picking up a small ornament. 'Wherever did he get this?' she frowned. 'I seem to recognise it as part of the junk I put in one of the attics. And this,' still acting in a proprietorial manner that set Thea's teeth on edge, she picked up and studied a framed photograph of three young men. 'Logan isn't all that sentimental, yet he keeps this?'

Thea felt like snatching the photograph from her. 'That's Mr Murray and his two brothers, I believe.'

The woman's face hardened cynically, marring its smooth perfection. 'You're quite right. As his elder brother's widow, I should know. I'm Ingrid Murray.'

'Oh.' Thea was startled, but did her best to hide it as she wasn't supposed to know anything about Logan's family. This woman must be James's wife. 'Oh,' she stammered again, 'I see. I'm sorry, Mrs Muray, I didn't realise who you were.'

Ingrid Murray shrugged. 'Why should you? My husband died four years ago and I went to live at Fort William. Logan took over here.'

Again, Thea wasn't sure what to say, if she was expected to say anything. She knew very little of what had taken place at Drumlarig after her mother left. After James died, had Logan put his sister-in-law out? If the estate was entailed then Drumlarig would automatically have come to Logan, but she couldn't imagine he would be that ruthless. 'Did you really want to leave Drumlarig?' she asked impulsively.

'No, not really.' Ingrid stared at Thea coolly. 'Logan did want me to stay, but I wasn't sure it would work.'

'There's Jamie, of course.'

'I agree,' Ingrid purred. 'He could do with a mother.'

'Miss Andrews!'

Both girls swung around. Logan stood in the doorway, anger tightening his strong features as his gaze clamped on Thea. She felt shaken. Why did he look so furious? She was certain she hadn't been indiscreet. It might have been difficult not to be, but so far she was sure she hadn't said anything out of place.

'Bring coffee to the library,' he ordered tersely, not deigning to explain his annoyance. He was too arrogant to explain anything, Thea thought waspishly, watching as he took his sister-in-law's arms and turned her away. 'How are you, Ingrid?' she heard him ask.

'It's Mr Murray's sister-in-law,' she replied to Martha's query, as she hurriedly rushed cups and saucers to a tray. Somehow Mrs Murray didn't look the mug and biscuits passed round in a packet type! She arranged several biscuits on a pretty plate, ignoring the freshly baked and still hot scones which Logan liked. They couldn't have everything in the library, she decided bitterly. They had each other!

After a few moments, in the way she had, Martha nodded sagely. 'That will be Miss Ingrid. She comes sometimes.'

'Why?' It mightn't be her business, but Thea was burning to know. Everything about Logan Murray, even the hard, ruthless, arrogant part of him, was fast becoming an obsession, if this was what was meant by scarcely being able to think of anything else.

'Why does she come here?' Martha repeated in her sharp, painstaking fashion. 'To see Himself, of course! She wouldn't mind being mistress of Drumlarig again, that I can tell you!'

'Then why did she go away?'

'She couldn't stay on and expect to sell the place, could she?'

In the act of pouring hot water into the heated pot, Thea glanced at Martha sharply. 'How could she sell Drumlarig? Wasn't it entailed?'

'No,' Martha shook her head, 'it was hers when Mr James died. Mr Logan had to buy it back—from her.'

'Mr Logan?'

'Yes,' Martha's small mouth pursed. 'She even sold the furniture. It's said that for everything she got not far short of a million, but she's still not satisfied.'

'The furniture?' Thea was concentrating so hard on this that she barely heard the sum of money Martha mentioned. 'So that's why there's so little in the library—why the other rooms are so bare!'

'Some of the books in the library were very old and valuable and Mr Logan didn't get back in time to save them. Or it might have been that he couldn't afford to, I forget. But it's unlikely that things will ever be the same again.'

Thea frowned. 'Where did Mr Murray buy the furniture he has now?'

'He didn't buy it,' Martha explained stiffly. 'It was in the attics, stuff which the auctioneering people said wasn't worth selling.'

That explained the extreme shabbiness! 'Couldn't Mr Murray have bought the old furniture back again, or got something new?'

'I think it took him all his time to buy the estate, Drumlarig and the other farms. She put it up for public auction, you know, all in one lot, and some foreigners were very keen to have it. The furniture, though, she sold privately beforehand.'

Thea, too intrigued to stop at this point, was too full of a kind of anguished sympathy for Logan to remember Martha's discretion wasn't to be relied on. She rushed on, 'Where was Logan while all this was happening?'

'Somewhere in foreign parts, making his fortune.' Martha spoke as if it was a wonder he had got back alive.

Unexpectedly, tears clogged Thea's throat as, incredibly, she seemed to share Martha's remembered anxiety. Without being entirely aware of what she was saying, she cried, 'If he was away so long why should he want to buy Drumlarig back?'

'Miss Andrews!'

Horrified, Thea gasped to see Logan striding in through the door. For the second time in about as many minutes she appeared to have maddened him. 'I'm just coming,' she gathered up her tray hastily, wondering how much he had heard.

'You'd better be,' he snapped, turning abruptly to depart again.

Martha wisely got on with her nap as Thea marched out

behind him. The coffee smelled good, but Thea hoped it
would poison their visitor. It was difficult to imagine how
Ingrid Murray had the nerve to show up here, after what
she had done, even if she had been within her legal rights.
Still, who was she, a mere housekeeper, to criticise, especially when Logan himself treated Ingrid like an honoured
guest. Besides, before the day was out she would probably
be on the receiving end of a lecture about poking her
nose in where it wasn't wanted, if the expression on
Logan's face was anything to go by!

She was. It began with Martha, no doubt looking after
her own interests, informing him that Thea had been asking questions again.

'About Miss Ingrid this time, Mr Logan.'

Despairingly, Thea made a weak attempt to save herself.
'I only asked because ...'

Logan rose from his lunch, which Thea had seen he
enjoyed, with a grim look on his face. He cut through
Thea's unhappy faltering like a knife through butter. 'If
you can spare me a few minutes in the library, Miss
Andrews, I'd be much obliged.'

Unhappily she followed him, not caring for the rigid set
of his broad shoulders. Was it only a few hours ago since
he had curved her head against them, almost devouring her
lips with his mouth? She must have dreamt it—if it
hadn't been for the searing response she could still feel
within her, she would never have believed it had happened. If she didn't watch out she might find herself in
love with him, and be worse off than ever.

Attempting to put all thoughts of love from her mind,
Thea tried to compose herself. Why couldn't Martha have
held her tongue? When she liked she could be a spiteful
old woman.

'Close the door,' Logan commanded from his usual
stance beside the fire. He stood with his back to it, his
strong legs braced, indicating the muscled strength of his

tall, powerful body. Standing there he looked capable of anything, certainly of reducing to size one foolish young girl.

Staring at him, as she did as she was told, Thea wondered how, even in his shabby old kilt, he managed to look like a king. He was full of black arrogance, despite his poverty, but there was something very fine about him which she couldn't ignore.

Her eyes still fixed on him, she said nervously, 'I didn't deliberately ask anything. It was only because of some comments your sister-in-law made, and—and one thing led to another.'

Logan's eyes examined her face, boring into her, making her draw back with an involuntary gasp which he ignored. He was well aware of his mounting power over her, or so it seemed to her, as she stood scorching beneath his cynical regard.

'She wasn't the only one making comments,' he said at last. 'Your own, about Jamie needing a mother, was very enlightening.'

'I never suggested that——'

'Thea!' his voice was low but suddenly explosive as he caught hold of her arms in a grip which hurt. 'Women have been suggesting that to me ever since Jamie's mother died. I'm immune to such hints, you'd only be wasting your time. I've had one wife and she was enough. I don't want another. Besides,' his eyes taunted, 'at twenty-nine I'm not sure whether you're too old or too young for me.'

That seemed to frighten her, somehow, and she reacted badly. Her face went white and she looked shaken. 'Jamie might prefer you to have a wife, though, rather than a succession of girl-friends. I expect there's been more than the doctor's daughter and your brother's wife?'

'My brother's wife?' His mouth tightened angrily while his eyes narrowed on her tormented face.

'Well,' Thea had the grace to feel ashamed, 'she didn't

actually say anything. She only implied that you wanted her to stay here.'

'Did she, indeed?'

Thea's temper rose quickly. 'You can take that cynical expression off your face! You believe every woman's after you, don't you? Well, if you think I'd like you for a husband, you can think again! I don't like men, Lo—I mean, Mr Murray.'

'Indeed?' he rejoined, reverting to lazy mockery, his eyes on the betraying pulse at the base of her throat. 'It appears, then, that neither of us is interested in a permanent relationship. All the same, my dear, in or out of marriage, I prefer an older woman who knows what she's doing.'

She wouldn't enter into anything with him, no matter how old she was! It must have been because his hands were hurting her arms, the way her heart was racing, which made her insist angrily, 'Why should age matter, if there's something between a man and woman?'

He smiled, this time with a touch of wry humour. 'You do believe in plunging in, do you not, just as you do through the rivers? You might be interested to know that Ingrid thinks you're too young to be working for me, let alone anything else. I had the greatest difficulty persuading her you're thirty.'

'Thirty?' Thea murmured apprehensively.

'Just so,' he agreed softly, releasing one of her arms to raise her rounded, babyish chin with a steely finger. 'I even find it difficult to believe myself, when I get this close. Not a line, such dewy freshness, all the bloom of extreme youthfulness.'

For a few more moments, breathless ones for Thea, he regarded her closely, before dropping his hands and moving away, unaware, she hoped, of her uneven breathing. His eyes went cold again, as he said cynically, 'Considering the kind of life you must have led, your look of innocence is amazing.'

She felt suddenly too miserable to cross words with him about that. Let him believe what he liked to believe!

'Another thing, Miss Andrews,' he went on curtly, 'I overheard you asking Martha why I should want to buy Drumlarig.'

Her face flushing scarlet, Thea exclaimed, 'It's surely no crime to ask a little thing like that!'

'I bought Drumlarig because I wanted it. Now are you satisfied?'

Silently, Thea nodded, not trusting herself to speak. It was a mistake, as she glared at him, to wonder where he had got the money from. Tightly she kept her mouth closed.

'That's right,' he mocked her approvingly. 'You're never too old to learn a little self-control. I didn't return here, you know, until I was thirty-two. In that time a man can accumulate quite a lot, if he likes to speculate and use his brains.'

Still she refused to comment, even while he appeared quite able to guess what she was thinking. Her voice trembled slightly when eventually she asked, 'Will that be all, Mr Murray?'

'Not quite. My mother and brother will be coming to spend Christmas and the New Year with us.' He frowned, looking at Thea steadily. 'After they've gone, I'm not sure that I'll continue to employ you, but there's no time now to make other arrangements.'

Unconsciously clenching her hands until the knuckles shone white, Thea tried to pretend she hadn't heard his last sentence. 'When will they be arriving?'

'Probably a day or two before Christmas. My mother has been living in Edinburgh since she left Drumlarig.'

Rather anxiously Thea gazed at him, wondering if she were capable of arranging a proper family Christmas. 'Do you have turkey for Christmas lunch, Mr Murray?'

'I expect so,' he sounded terse. 'Do what you like, as

long as you don't bother me. This time you have my permission.'

Within what limits? Warily, she watched him. 'Jamie
would like a tree, and so would I.' This last was true, but
she really tacked it on so he wouldn't think she would find
it a nuisance.

Having half expected an abrupt refusal, she was surprised when he merely shrugged. She could have sworn
there was even a slight smile on his lips. 'I've already told
you to do what you like, more or less. Now, I've work to
do.'

He turned to his desk and, gratified, Thea left him. He
hadn't refused to have a tree in the house. He'd just dismissed it, along with everything else, which she supposed
he imagined a good housekeeper should be able to take
care of. Well, he needn't worry that she might be short
of initiative. Already so many plans were beginning to
formulate in her mind, she didn't know which to concentrate on first. With a small click of triumph, she closed the
door.

CHAPTER SIX

THEA laid her plans carefully. That evening, after Logan had gone out and Jamie and Martha had gone to bed, she rang her solicitor. As he was an old family friend she had his home number and knew he wouldn't mind her ringing him there. He had, in fact, begged her to keep in touch, to ring him anytime. He was happy to know she was well and occupying herself in exploring Scotland. Yes, he would be delighted to transfer some money to a nearby bank for her. She could almost feel his relief that she didn't mention giving it away again.

About that, Thea now had other ideas, although she wasn't sure yet how she was to put them into practice. Her mind, still confused on some issues, warned her she would be wiser to proceed with caution. From hating Logan Murray and despising his meanness, her feelings were rapidly changing to ones of great sympathy.

Now she wanted to help him—and Jamie, using the money she had recently scorned for this purpose. Hourly new dreams were born and grew, beginning with the house, with which she was most familiar. She saw it refurnished from top to bottom, deep carpets everywhere. Strangely, she wasn't at all concerned about such things for herself, but Jamie's bedroom was so cold, it's floor boasting only one small bare rug. She could get all sorts of things for him. Cupboards in which he could put his books—books to put in them. A new transistor, which he longed for, even a new pony, a livelier one than the one he rode at present. Old Dusty could easily be pensioned off.

But it was on Logan that her dreams centred. Out on the farm he was badly in need of new machinery. What he had seemed mostly old and worn out. The horse he rode was a huge, wild-looking creature with a fearful temper. Thea, who prided herself on being able to ride almost anything, could never see herself up on that. That could be replaced, along with all the rest. She didn't want Duncan finding Logan thrown, or trampled to death. The very thought of it made her grow cold, strengthening her resolutions.

There seemed no end to what she could do. She didn't come into the bulk of her money until she was twenty-five, but what she had would do more good here than lying idle in the bank. The snag was Logan; he would never agree. Thea liked to think he would, even while every instinct warned her he would not. He had so much pride. Far too much, she found herself saying aloud, and fiercely, when she couldn't think of a way of getting around it.

After days of solid thinking, which was making her absentminded to a noticeable degree, she decided she must wait and see. With renewed optimism she felt certain something would turn up. There was always a way, Gran used to say, if one waited long enough.

Meanwhile, Thea secretly went on doing what she could. She went to Fort William, borrowing Logan's car as he said the Land Rover wasn't suitable. Like a lot of other things at Drumlarig, it was old and might break down, and it might be hours before she could get in touch with him, if it did.

'I've checked the car over,' a slight smile relaxed the corners of his mouth. 'Are you sure you can manage on your own?'

'I'm a modern girl, remember.' For one heart-stopping moment Thea thought he was about to offer to accompany her. Some part of her considered an outing with Logan Murray wistfully, but today she had too many private things to do.

'That's just it,' she was surprised to hear him retort

rather grimly, 'I don't believe you are, not completely.'

Swiftly she turned her head so he wouldn't see the colour tinting her cheeks. Somehow he made it sound like a compliment, and she wasn't used to any real kindness from him.

'Will you be all right, Thea?'

He even sounded anxious. 'There's no reason why I shouldn't be.' Because her heart was suddenly pounding it was an effort to smile casually. Then her smile faded as she met his eyes pleadingly. 'You won't forget to fetch Jamie, will you?'

'If I can manage it, but don't spend your day worrying about us.' He seemed as if he had something more to say, but instead he changed his mind and left her.

Warmed by his concern and the intent look he bent on her as he turned away, Thea spent quite a satisfactory day. The massive flanks of Ben Nevis stood out clear through the retreating morning mist as she drove towards Fort William, making her think of other lonely if beautiful places, such as Rannoch Moor and Glencoe, that famous part of Scotland where the Macdonalds had been put to death by fire and the sword in 1692.

Until she came to live here, this had only been something learnt about at school, during long, often boring lessons. Now that she felt part of it a new appreciation was creeping into her very bones. No one, she thought, could live here, or even visit, without becoming aware of the incredible beauty and majesty of their surroundings, but there was more to it than that. It was a land steeped in history, a lot of it tragic, but the fundamental, courageous spirit of the people still prevailed. Didn't she feel it everywhere—something which had triumphantly survived the cruel centuries.

On her second visit to Fort William, set in the centre of wild, magnificent country, she found she liked it even better than her first. Even in winter it had its appeal. The High

Street at this time of the year was uncrowded, the shops
well stocked by any standards, and gay.

The money she had asked for had come through and,
after establishing her identity, she was able to draw what
she required. For almost the first time since receiving her
legacy, Thea enjoyed spending it. This was, she suddenly
realised, because she was spending it on people she really
liked.

Almost, she thought, loved. She did love Jamie and suspected she was well on the way towards loving his father;
useless to try and hide it from herself any longer. Logan
might be ill-tempered and arrogant and determined to
keep her firmly in her place, but it was impossible to deny
his growing attraction for her. Twice he had kissed her,
both times unintentionally and in a manner that had
scarcely been complimentary, yet she seemed to crave to be
in his arms again. Why was it, she wondered unhappily,
that she was either longing for him or hating him? How
did a girl decide which of the two emotions was real?

Since Gran and she had had to leave their lovely home
in the country, after Thea's cousin had taken it over, after
their grandfather's death, she had never felt able to settle
anywhere else. At Drumlarig, huge, old and cold as it was,
she felt happier than she had ever been before. Wistfully,
she thought she could live at Drumlarig for the rest of her
life, given a little encouragement. If she didn't get that, and
her time here was limited, then she must just be grateful
for each day.

For Jamie's Christmas present she found a small radio
and an electric train set, to which he could add. There were
plenty of empty rooms at Drumlarig to accommodate the
latter. Then some books. Knowing his taste, having read a
lot to him and with him, she knew exactly what he liked
and enjoyed. She would have bought him more, but dared
not, having no wish to arouse Logan's animosity or sus-
picions.

She did buy Jamie several articles of clothing which he was badly in need of, and which she could smuggle into his wardrobe without his father knowing.

For Logan she bought socks, astonished at herself for the trouble she took over choosing them. Never having bought socks for a man before, she had no idea there were so many kinds and colours. It wasn't until she told a helpful saleslady that the man she was buying them for usually wore a kilt that she managed to get what she wanted. As the woman wrapped them up, Thea sighed, wishing she could have found him something more out of the ordinary. But at least he couldn't object to such a sober and uninteresting present.

She got Martha a warm shawl for her shoulders, hoping she didn't know the difference between cashmere and something cheaper, and added a pair of furry slippers. For Logan's mother and brother she purchased large boxes of chocolates, feeling sure they would share them with the rest of the family.

Again with the intention of smuggling it into the house secretly, she spent quite a lot on Christmassy items, which included food and decorations. The floor of the drawing room might look bare, but the room would be vastly improved with the help of a few streamers and other things which she had found upstairs.

At last there only remained some clothes to buy for herself. She had plenty in her flat in London, but this didn't solve her immediate problem. There was no one she could really trust to pack them up and send them to her. To do that she would have to give an address and for the time being she didn't want anyone to know where she was. It was too easy to imagine Jerry arriving, a smear of triumph on his lips, on the doorstep!

Keeping a wary eye on the darkening sky, Thea quickly visited several good dress shops. Because she had left herself with little time, if she wanted to get home before dark, she didn't take too much time over what she was buying. Not until it came to a dress for Christmas Day. For this she wanted something special and eventually decided on a soft, rose-coloured gown which she saw, as soon as she tried it on, was very flattering. With her hair freshly washed and shining, and a little pink lipstick on her nicely shaped mouth, even Logan Murray might look twice.

Arriving back at Drumlarig, she could have skipped for joy to find that Logan had left to pick Jamie up and also to make one or two calls in the village. Martha told her they wouldn't be home until about six.

Long before then, Thea had her parcels unpacked and put away. Martha, happily chewing her way through a large box of sweets Thea had bought for her, didn't seem to notice that Thea made several journeys to and fro from the car. By six, Thea had a good meal ready, for once not caring that Logan might well wonder how she managed to produce anything so splendid on what he gave her.

She wasn't foolish enough to hide everything. When Jamie returned she kissed him and showed him what she had got for the tree. Although Logan watched, narrowed eyes glinting, he didn't pass a comment or ask any questions. His eyes might momentarily have been bleak, but for once he raised no objections when Jamie impulsively hugged Thea, as he shared her excitement. Their sparkling, flushed young faces seemed, if anything, to afford him some small satisfaction. After dinner, on which he congratulated her enigmatically, he got up to go to the library, but before he went he stared at her intently for a few pulse-racing seconds, as closely as he had done earlier in the day.

Dizzy from the apparent success of her shopping trip to Fort William, Thea felt she was riding on the crest of a wave. She had no idea that her luck was about to run out. Next morning, the day before Jamie's grandmother was due to arrive, she iced the cake she had baked the week before. Having been told by Martha that Mrs Murray always brought Christmas puddings, she tactfully didn't try to make these. For one thing she wasn't sure if she could have managed it, although she had seen them made often enough.

She had also been told that Christmas in Scotland wasn't usually celebrated as enthusiastically as it was in England, but Logan did seem to be making some concessions. In the early afternoon he brought in a tree, a rather beautiful one about eight feet in height. Together, he and Thea erected it. It was difficult to decide where to put it and at last they voted for the hall, where Thea thought it would give a festive appearance to the whole house.

Thea, her cheeks hot from exertion, was very conscious of Logan beside her. He was as taciturn as ever, the cynical twist of his lips betraying, if silently, his inner doubts over his own sanity, but most of the time he seemed disposed to please her. Once their hands touched, which brought their eyes leaping together and her heart began thudding. It was a moment in time, a prelude to arms reaching out, mouths clinging, urgent with desire. Yet the moment passed, as he shifted his position, as though it had never happened.

Trembling and feeling ashamed of herself, Thea said, 'I'll sweep up the mess, then Jamie and I will begin decorating after tea.' She knew she spoke breathlessly, but she couldn't help it. She didn't look at Logan.

'Would you like me to go and get him again?'

It was so like the kind of thing a man might offer to do for his busy wife at Christmas time that Thea felt tears spring to the back of her eyes. To hide them, she smiled quickly. 'Oh, no. It's good of you to offer, but I've an order I want to pick up at the shop and there are a few things I forgot to put on it. I'll manage.'

He smiled down at her. 'Thirty isn't so very old,' he teased, 'but you seem to have retained a lot of your teenage enthusiasm?'

Looking away quickly, Thea floundered in her attempt to divert him without committing herself. 'Don't—don't you like women of thirty, Mr Murray?'

Again he grinned. 'I'm beginning to wonder, but don't tempt me, Miss Andrews. I'm certainly in no doubt about women's tricks, no matter what their age. And if I'm ever willing to appear taken in by any one of you it's seldom on my own doorstep.'

With a small grimace, that she tried to make indifferent, Thea excused herself. That was plain enough, whichever way one cared to look at it!

If it hadn't been for this exchange, which she had found disturbing, she wondered afterwards if she might have been able to avoid the accident that happened.

Driving to the village from Drumlarig, the road twisted, often tortuously, but as there were few hedges the view was seldom completely obstructed. Once in the village, however, the vista changed. Several of the narrow roads leading into it appeared to come around completely blind corners, on to the main street. It was from out of one of these side roads that another motorist raced, just as Thea was approaching.

As she hadn't time to stop, she couldn't do anything to avoid a collision. Neither could the other driver. It was a man and he hit her side-on, on the side she was sitting. With the impact she was thrown straight across the front seats, while the Land Rover spun out of control. Fortunately, perhaps, at that very spot was a high hedge, against which the Land Rover finished up drunkenly.

Thea didn't know what happened immediately after this as she was knocked half unconscious. Hazily she became aware of a lot of noise; of men shouting, of engines being switched off, of other cars arriving. But when she tried to move everything kept receding and going black. She felt no pain. There was only an odd inability to pull herself together.

Then someone was easing her carefully to a more comfortable position, while a man's voice which she didn't recognise kept on insisting that the accident had been entirely his fault. He seemed full of regret and would allow no one to touch her until a doctor came. There was a certain kindness in his voice that Thea found oddly comforting, even if she couldn't open her eyes to look at him. She found it impossible to even tell them who she was, yet when Drumlarig was mentioned, and Logan, she was filled with a vague alarm.

In another few minutes the doctor arrived with Logan. Logan was furious and making no attempt to hide it, though Thea wasn't sure who he was angry with. Anxiously, as the doctor probed and a small groan escaped her, she tried to explain, but was told sharply by Logan to shut up.

After Doctor Stewart completed a brief examination and said it was all right to do so, Logan lifted her gently, carrying her to the doctor's house, which was only a few yards away. Carefully he laid her on the couch in the surgery, then brushed back her tumbled hair with what to Thea seemed surprisingly tender fingers, before leaving her, at Doctor Stewart's request, for a further examination.

'I'll be back,' she heard him informing Doctor Stewart curtly, 'after I've given McLean a piece of my mind!'

A short while later, when she regained her senses completely, she was relieved to learn she was suffering from little more than concussion.

'You've had a slight blow on the side of your head,' the doctor said. 'You've been very fortunate. After a good night's rest you should be as good as new, but I'll take another look at you in the morning.'

'I feel all right,' she tried to get a better grip on herself, 'just a bit sick.'

'McLean ought to be shot,' the doctor grunted, Thea thought to himself. 'One of these days he'll kill somebody.' He mixed her something in a glass and passed it to her. 'This will help.' He assisted her to drink it when she found it difficult to hold the glass.

She didn't know who McLean was, nor was she very interested. All she could think of, when she managed to sit up, was Logan and Jamie. 'Jamie?' she gasped. 'I was on my way to meet him!'

'That's been taken care of,' Doctor Stewart assured her.

'Was Logan very mad?' she whispered, sinking back again.

Doctor Stewart actually smiled. 'I hardly think he would be with you, but I wouldn't be in McLean's shoes for a fortune.'

'I don't expect he meant to harm anyone,' she murmured absently, her eyes on the door. 'Where's Lo—I mean Mr Murray now? I'd like to go home.'

'He's dealing with the police. He'll be here shortly,' Irene Stewart spoke from the doorway, 'I'm afraid he isn't very pleased. His Land Rover looks as if it might be out of action for some time. Poor Logan!'

'Scarcely Miss Andrews' fault, my dear.' The doctor's bushy brows drew together.

If Irene's chosen role was that of Job's comforter, she cleverly disguised it. 'I'm only going by appearances, Daddy,' she rejoined sweetly, casting Thea a mocking glance. 'Logan doesn't seem kindly disposed towards anybody, and I imagine this goes for his housekeeper too.'

Thea felt the other girl's spite, but was too weary to retaliate. Besides, what she said might be quite true. In fact she was forced to agree when, a short while later, Logan came for her. If she was sick and shaken, she felt worse when she saw his face. It was positively thunderous. His face was grim, there was a white line running from his nose to his mouth and she could almost feel the effort he made to control the anger smouldering within him.

Not able to find the immediate self-possession to say much, she tried to mollify him, 'I'm sorry about the Land Rover, Mr Murray.'

'That wasn't your fault,' he acknowledged tersely.

Irene suggested quickly, 'If Miss Andrews would like to rest a little longer, Logan, she'd be very welcome. Perhaps you'd like a cup of tea?'

He thanked her but refused. 'Jamie's waiting outside in the car, Irene. I'd rather get straight back.'

Thea got to her feet too quickly and swayed. Doctor Stewart steadied her. 'Perhaps you'd better carry Miss Andrews, Logan.'

'She can walk.'

The doctor shot him a puzzled glance but said nothing further. Thea's face was chalk white, he could feel her shaking. He helped her to the car himself.

Logan opened the door and slammed it behind her. When Jamie began unexpectedly to cry, he snapped at him, 'That's enough of that, my lad. Miss Andrews will survive. Some people have a remarkable talent for it.'

The street was silent, no one in sight, as though Logan's anger had swept through them as well, scaring away any curious spectators. Thea shuddered, suddenly as cold as ice. Something was very wrong, she could feel it.

Jamie shrank in his corner, clearly bewildered. Logan said nothing. Miss Andrews will survive the accident but nothing else, his black silence seemed to say as he swung the car around abruptly and started back to Drumlarig.

With the sharp turn, Thea lost her precarious balance and fell against Jamie's seat. An audible sob rising to her throat, she straightened with difficulty. Although she must be responsible, in a way, for crippling his Land Rover, she wouldn't have believed Logan could be so unfeeling. Surely his Land Rover wasn't that important? While she wasn't ill or injured, she had had a fright and no matter how she tried she couldn't pull herself together any faster. Having never been involved in a car accident before, she had had no idea it could affect one like this. Tears, which she couldn't seem to stop, ran down her cheeks. Jamie, his own eyes still brimming, passed her his handkerchief.

'Thanks,' she breathed noisily, taking it from him, an act which seemed to comfort him as much as it did her. Logan's back was rigid and didn't relax all the way to Drumlarig.

On the paved forefront, he slammed out of the car and disappeared into the house, while Jamie stared after his infuriated father, as bewildered as Thea. Thea, attempting to reassure the boy, got out of the car herself, promptly falling on the muddy ground as her feet slid from under her.

'Can you help me, Jamie?' She was sobbing in earnest now and could make no further attempt to hide it. On top of the fright she had got, all her hopes and dreams had collapsed and there was anguish in her heart.

Jamie, as though determined to prove himself a man again, stopped whimpering and squared his young shoulders. Gravely he took his handkerchief back and rubbed the dirt from Thea's hands. 'Of course I'll help you,' he said.

'Just to my room,' she said gratefully, as he kept a tight hold of her hand. 'If I rest for an hour or two I'll be all right. Doctor Stewart said so.'

'Are you sure?' he whispered anxiously.

'Of course,' she even managed a weak smile. 'I'll be down soon to get your dinner. And remember your grandmother will be here tomorrow.'

'I don't think I care for Granny as much as you,' he replied flatly. 'Although she is nice.'

In her room she sent him away. She would have a wash, then lie down, she said.

Jamie looked doubtful but did as he was told. If Martha was making tea, he would bring her some up, he said.

Jamie's obvious concern touched Thea so much that when he was gone she was conscious of a curious choking sensation. Without bothering to wash she fell on her bed, burying her face in her pillows. Her temple, which she had caught against the steering wheel, throbbed, the ache going through her whole head.

A moment later the door opened and Logan walked in. Thea, scarcely able to see for pain, jerked upright. She knew she must look a sight, but she didn't care. Nothing seemed to matter any more. She was aching and she felt miserable. 'What do you want now?' she cried bitterly.

'An explanation,' he replied unfeelingly, his hands just as unsympathetic as he swung her feet to the floor, forcing her to sit on the side of the bed.

'An explanation?' The room swung around, but when she involuntarily clutched his arm to steady herself, he jerked his arm away.

'Pull yourself together, Miss Andrews,' he ground out, 'unless you want me to do it for you. I don't believe anyone as capable of deception as you are has many weak spots, not even physically.'

'I ...' She made a great effort to do as she was told, although the brilliance of his burning eyes almost scorched her. 'The car came straight at me, Logan, straight out of the road end. I couldn't do a thing ...' Suddenly, in the small, weighted silence that followed, she realised this wasn't the explanation he was after. 'What are you trying to say?' she whispered apprehensively.

'I saw the police,' he enlightened her.

Painfully, Thea nodded. 'I—I suppose they would be there, but it wasn't my fault.'

'They know that. The evidence was clear enough,' he paused, his eyes ruthless on her white face. 'They had to check your driving licence.'

Again she nodded numbly, staring, in bewilderment, back at him, as he went on harshly.

'I found it in your handbag, which was lying on the seat beside you. You were in no condition to show them anything and I thought it would save you any further worry if they looked at it there and then.'

'Yes, of course.' It made sense. It was standard procedure, she supposed, in most cases, and she always carried her driving licence with her. Then, as he waited grimly, she gasped at him in horror, 'My driving licence ... Oh, no!'

'It's quite in order,' his dark face contorted savagely. 'Quite in order.'

There was a low vibrancy in his voice as ruthlessly he grasped hold of her shoulders. He seemed to be hiding some powerful emotion. Terrified, Thea suddenly sagged, wondering if he knew, or if she could bluff her way out. 'Why are you mad, then?'

'Mad!' his grip tightened cruelly. 'I'm so mad, Thea, I'd like to say things not fit for your ears. How old did you tell me you were?'

The fight went completely out of her at that. 'You mean, you saw? You know?'

He didn't spare her. 'Your passport was there, too. I only needed to glance at that, but it all added up to you.'

Unable to look at him, she felt shocked and ill, but she knew she had been wrong to deceive him. 'The—the police?' she whispered, her lips trembling.

'Oh,' he laughed harshly, 'they'll be discreet enough, but how long, do you think, before the news gets out? Before the whole district knows that the new housekeeper at Drumlarig is little more than twenty years old?'

'I'm sorry, Logan,' his terse anger was frightening, 'but are you sure anyone will take much notice? After all, I'm only an employee.'

'This afternoon, half the village must have heard you

calling me Logan, as I carried you into the doctor's.'

'I couldn't have known what I was saying.'

'Well, I do—and so do they,' he cut in curtly. 'You appeared to think it would give the wrong impression if I carried you, but you probably did that yourself by gabbling my name.'

She couldn't keep repeating that she couldn't have realised what she was saying. Her eyes fixed on his, clouded with misery, a silent misery which was eating away at her heart.

'You knew, of course, that if I'd had any idea of your true age I'd have thrown you out that first day! You're full of tricks, aren't you? Instead of a down-and-out little brat on the run from God knows what, you posed as someone old enough to know what they were doing.'

'But—I—we haven't done anything.'

He ignored her tearful bewilderment. 'I've had several housekeepers, Thea, that I'll admit, but not one of them a day under forty. If they didn't stay long, with the majority it was because the isolation and various other aspects of the house didn't suit them. Maybe I was unlucky, but they all went. That's why I decided to take a risk with you. Thirty was still too young, but not unforgivably so. And, as far as Jamie was concerned, the situation was getting desperate.'

Hesitantly Thea swallowed. His voice was so curt and cold it made her shiver. 'I may as well confess, Logan, I didn't come to Scotland with the specific intention of looking for any particular sort of work. When I came here you were ill and I liked Jamie. He was like the young brother I would have liked but never had, or perhaps,' her cheeks coloured faintly, 'the son I hope to have one day. I knew you wouldn't let me stay if I told you I was twenty, even almost twenty-one, and one lie seemed to lead to another.'

'As always,' he agreed harshly. 'Tell one and you find you have to tell a hundred others.'

Not quite, she wanted to say unhappily, not daring to risk being forced to explain anything else. Not at the moment. 'I suppose you'll want me to leave immediately.'

He smiled grimly, a smile which Thea didn't find reassuring, although suddenly a lot of his anger seemed to leave him. Broodingly, his eyes rested on her. 'Unfortunately it won't be possible for you to leave immediately. I'm afraid you'll have to stay until after Christmas. My mother's coming in the morning, remember, and she won't be prepared to take over at a moment's notice. But more important, you'll stay a little longer for Jamie's sake. I won't have his Christmas ruined. He's going to be heartbroken enough as it is.'

Steeped in misery, Thea stared down at her hands. For Jamie's sake and his mother's, but not his. In spite of her growing love for Jamie, she had a hysterical desire to refuse to stay. Yet even as she opened her mouth to do this, she found herself surrendering to something she didn't understand, the pressure of Logan's will over her own. 'If you really want me to stay,' she found herself murmuring weakly, 'I will. As I said, I have nowhere else to go.'

'Yes, that's what I want.' He spoke so grimly she was startled, but when she looked up quickly his eyes were on the window.

A cold, damp wind was blowing, making the thin cotton curtains tremble at the edges. With an impatient sigh Logan strode over to close the window, drawing the curtains across it, his frown deepening, as if he had just realised their obvious inability to keep out the December cold. 'There's an electric fire somewhere,' he glanced back at the shivering girl. 'It's like a morgue in here, which can't be good for you. If you wait a few minutes I'll see what I can find.'

As he left the room, Thea continued to shiver, but it wasn't wholly from cold. A lot of it stemmed from the thought of having to leave Drumlarig. Her reprieve was only to be of a short duration. Apprehensively she gazed at the door through which Logan had disappeared. He was a strange man, with his varying moods which could change so rapidly from cold anger to kindness, but she loved him. More than anyone or anything. The knowledge of this love, hitting her like a blow, left her trembling. She couldn't mistake it. It was something she had never experienced before and never would again, for anyone but Logan Murray. Love for him moved through her, making her alive, in a way she would never have believed possible, but very vulnerable. She might feel she was suffering now, but she suspected there was worse to come, as Logan would never see her as a desirable woman.

When she went back to London, she would meet other men, men who weren't all villains like Jerry Banks. A girl who lived in a luxury penthouse was not usually lonely for want of attention. There were men who could keep her in style compared with Logan Murray, but he was the only man she could ever marry. It was his love that she wanted, his passion. She wanted to have his children, as well as wanting to look after Jamie. There was room for any amount of children at Drumlarig. Jamie needn't ever be lonely again. Above all there was Logan, but unhappily he had no time for her. Nothing she could do now was going to alter the bad opinion he had formed of her. It would probably be a waste of time even to try.

When he returned, carrying a large portable fire, she was still sitting where he had left her. As he plugged in the fire and a glow of instant warmth began penetrating the room, she was startled when he smiled at her. True, it was a smile which didn't give much away, but to Thea, with a strange hunger in her breast, it was better than nothing.

'Can you manage to get undressed and into bed?' he asked, his mouth tightening, as he noticed the extreme paleness of her face.

'I have to get dinner . . .'

'Not tonight.' He came nearer again, but now the hand on her shoulder was gentle. 'Thea, I'm sorry. I didn't intend hurting you. It was the shock of learning your true age, on top of the shock of your accident. I should have guessed about your age, but I never did care for being deceived.'

His apology surprised her. Intuitively, she guessed it had surprised Logan as well, as he seemed for a moment faintly disturbed. 'Logan . . .?' she began hesitantly.

'No more, Thea.' He wouldn't allow her to go on, 'Let's forget about it until after Christmas, shall we? A homeless waif doesn't always act sensibly, I suppose, and I'd almost forgotten what it's like to be down to nearly my last penny.'

Closing her eyes, Thea felt guilt of another kind swamping her. Was there to be no end to it? She must tell him everything. She might be an orphan, with no one who really cared for her, but she certainly wasn't a penniless, homeless waif. And she should be ashamed of herself for letting him continue to think so!

CHAPTER SEVEN

SEARCHING around, her wide anxious eyes eloquently expressing much of her inner torment, if not the exact source of it, Thea almost jumped when Logan's hand tightened on her shoulder.

'No more tonight, Thea, there's a good girl. Here,' he bent down, 'take your dressing-gown to the bathroom and see if you can manage to wash that mud off. I'll wait here until I see you're safely in bed. Then Jamie and I will bring you something on a tray. Martha can stir herself for once, it won't do her any harm.'

Hopelessly Thea held back the flood of explanations which he left her in no doubt he wasn't prepared to listen to. It was there in the firm implacability of his face as he stood, his arms folded now, watching her.

'You don't have to go to all this trouble,' she protested weakly.

'I want you to feel better in the morning, Thea.'

So she would be quite able to look after his guests! Next morning, as she climbed stiffly out of bed, Thea thought she saw the purpose behind Logan's kindness of the night before. His mother was coming today and he wanted her visit to proceed smoothly. It was important to him that no domestic crisis should be there to interrupt his normal routine. If he was willing to bring his housekeeper her supper on a tray it was because his day's work was over.

Last night, as he had threatened, he remained in her room until she had washed and got into bed. There had been nothing for it but to discard her dressing-gown in front of him and pretend her slim, bare legs were invisible under the lacy hem of her short cotton nightdress. Her arms and a lot of her shoulders had been bare, too, as she had only brought things which took up little space in her rucksack. Logan hadn't appeared to notice. He had been so matter-of-fact, he might have been her grandmother. Only momentarily did an expression flick through his dark eyes which hadn't been grandmotherish at all.

He and Jamie brought her a bowl of soup and an omelette. Jamie had hugged her again and told her she looked pretty, something she had found difficult to believe with the bruise over her eye beginning to show and her long hair hanging damp and straight. He had looked happier, though, especially when Logan smiled at her. He was convinced that his father had forgiven Thea for damaging the Land Rover. He hadn't known that that wasn't the cause of what was wrong. Jamie's pleasure in her recovery had been so moving, she didn't have the heart to tell him about that. She would still have to go, even if Logan had temporarily decided he had nothing to lose by being kind to her.

This morning she was still haunted by the confession she ought to have made, about being here as a child and not being penniless, but suddenly there didn't seem much point any more. It could make no difference to her ultimate departure and might only serve to embarrass Logan further. If he knew he might feel forced to ask her to stay and it might make him even angrier than he was now. Whichever way she looked at it, it might be wiser to stay silent.

Logan went to meet his mother at Fort William as she was coming by train from Edinburgh. He took an excited Jamie with him and while they were gone Thea got busy. She was amazed that she felt surprisingly well. Her brow was a little sore and discoloured, her left elbow and arm slightly stiff where she had fallen on them, but all her other aches had disappeared.

'Youth,' Logan had explained sardonically, when she had remarked on it. 'At your age a bump or two seldom has any lasting effect.'

She had felt too raw, over what seemed a deliberate dig over her lack of years, to respond very gracefully as he made her sit down at the kitchen table and drink the cup of tea he poured out for her.

His face had been as expressionless as it usually was, unless he was angry, when it was sometimes even more so, but he did seem to realise she had age on her mind. Before he left for the station, while Jamie was climbing into the car, he came back to the hall to speak to her.

'When my mother asks how old you are, as she will do, I should tell her the truth, if I were you. She won't be as willing to be deceived as I was.'

What had Logan meant by that? There was no time to do more than wonder briefly. She had a lot to do and no energy to spare for anything but work. Once she was properly on her feet she found the accident had shaken her more than she liked to admit.

Despite this continuing lassitude, she had everything under control, even the dining-room table elegantly laid before Logan returned with his mother. He was back! She heard car doors slam, breaking the cold, rather eerie silence of midday. Jamie's voice came, still excited, then a woman's, then Logan's deep one, answering.

Thea, crossing the hall to see if any help was needed, felt strung up with high tension. Her heart was thumping with nervousness; she hadn't thought this moment would mean so much to her. She was anxious to see if she remembered Mrs Murray, but even more anxious to discover if Mrs Murray should remember her. The latter being much the more likely, Thea couldn't bring herself to wait to find out. She might feel like a prisoner hurrying to their own execution, but she couldn't stop herself.

Mrs Murray came through the door before Thea

reached it. 'Logan?' Mrs Murray was beginning, when she caught sight of Thea. Her face blank with surprise, she paused when confronted by a slender young girl, quite lovely with her fair hair and grey eyes, for all the huge apron which covered the greater part of her soft blue dress. 'Good heavens!' she exclaimed involuntarily, almost exactly as her daughter-in-law had done. 'This can't be ... Is this ...? Logan, are you ...?'

With a completely expressionless face, Logan cut off the half-finished sentences. 'This is Thea Andrews, Mother.' As he looked at Thea, catching the extreme anguish in her dilated eyes, he frowned.

He hadn't introduced her as his housekeeper, but it was obvious that he had explained who she was before they arrived. Thea murmured 'good morning' and, because she was so terribly shaken, did her best to copy Logan's deadpan expression. She didn't hold out her hand. Half extended, she withdrew it, fearing to give the impression of that of a hostess welcoming a guest.

Anxiously, while Mrs Murray appeared to be searching for her voice, Thea stared at her. All morning she had waited to see the woman who had been so kind to her mother, but now she was here she didn't even recognise her. Mrs Logan's face was kind, her skin still smooth if slightly lined. Her eyes weren't lacking in humour even if, at the moment, it wasn't too obvious. They were the same colour as Logan's, but never so cold, and like him she had a kind of presence which wasn't usually forgotten. Yet there was not one feature that Thea could recollect.

Mrs Logan, seldom having been beaten by silence in her life, managed to reply normally to Thea's tentative greetings, and the occasion was saved by old Martha's hobbling appearance in the kitchen doorway. At least, Thea thought it was saved until Martha spoke.

'Hello, Miss Sarah. What do you think of Mr Logan's new housekeeper? I knew you'd be taken aback.'

A guilty flush staining her cheeks, Thea dropped her burnished head. She had wanted Mrs Murray to like her, but Martha's perky query would put an end to any such possibility.

Surprise made her glance up quickly as Mrs Murray smiled warmly and began walking towards the old woman. 'How are you, Martha?' she asked—only that. No comment on her remark about Thea. Thea felt oddly ashamed that she had decided Mrs Murray would judge her on Martha's word alone.

Whatever Mrs Murray's private thoughts on the matter she was apparently keeping them to herself, for the time being, anyway. She was a woman, Thea was soon to realise, who never jumped to too hasty conclusions, although she set great store by the fitness of things. If she privately considered Thea too young to be Logan's housekeeper, she wasn't small-minded enough to condemn her on everything else. Quite openly she praised the lunch Thea had prepared with such care. She was as generous over that as she was about the freshness of her bedroom and the comfort of the drawing-room.

'You've made quite a difference, my dear,' she said, when Thea brought in coffee.

Logan stretched his long legs as he lay back in one of the deep chairs and didn't take his eyes from Thea's face. He's wondering what I'm going to say to that, she thought, suddenly angry. His grim surveillance was becoming something difficult to endure as there was no kindness in his prolonged scrutiny.

Thea, turning her straight back on him, haltingly explained to his mother how she had tried moving some of the furniture around a bit. Duncan had helped her carry a few comfortable chairs from a room at the end of the passage, which no one seemed to use. 'I hope you don't mind?' she finished diffidently.

'No, my dear child. Of course not—why should I?' Mrs

Murray sighed heavily, though Thea thought not bitterly. 'It's not my business what happens any more at Drumlarig, but it must have made a lot of work for you.'

'No, it's been fun,' she tried but failed to keep the eagerness from her voice. 'I like Drumlarig.' She didn't look at Logan but could almost feel the speculation in his eyes.

Jamie said, before his grandmother could reply. 'Thea and I are going to decorate the tree this afternoon. That is if Father says she's able to.'

'Oh, yes,' Mrs Murray was contrite, 'my son's just been telling me about your unfortunate accident, Miss Andrews. You've quite recovered, I hope? Ian McLean is pleasant enough, but he always did drive too fast.'

The telephone rang. Logan went out to answer it. When he came back, he said, 'That was McLean, with more apologies. He wanted to speak to you, Thea, but I refused, on your behalf.'

Feeling an indignant flush rising to her cheeks at such high-handedness, Thea exclaimed, 'I wouldn't have minded speaking to him, Logan! I—er—I mean Mr Murray,' she trailed off miserably. It had been a mistake to use his christian name in his mother's presence. She saw Mrs Murray glance at her sharply before looking at Logan.

Thea tried to hide her mounting confusion with further argument. Staring at Logan, she began, 'If he wanted to apologise personally, then I think you should have let him. I wish ...'

'Your wishes, in this case, couldn't be considered,' Logan returned flatly. 'You must allow me to know best.'

'I don't see ...'

'Thea!'

His eyes held hers until she began to tremble. Mutinously silent, she turned away, furious with him, yet having no particular desire to speak to Ian McLean. It must be the strange antagonism she felt towards Logan which made her long to defy him in some way. Which was foolish, when she would be leaving Drumlarig after Christmas.

Logan's brother didn't come, after all. When Mrs Murray came to the kitchen for a cup of tea, which she had insisted she would have there instead of in the drawing-room, she said she had just had a call from him. He had decided to go abroad, at the last minute. She didn't say she was disappointed, but Thea noticed the strain on her face. Quietly she poured Mrs Murray a cup of tea, adding a good spoonful of sugar before placing it beside her as the woman sat down rather heavily at the table. Her silent gesture seemed to forge a link of sympathy and from that moment on the two of them were friends.

Thea learnt that, in Edinburgh, Mrs Murray looked after her sister who was more or less bedridden. As they were both widows this usually worked out fairly well, but it presented problems when Mrs Murray had to go away. She had only managed a break this Christmas because some of her sister's husband's relations had agreed to come and stay with her.

'I was longing to see Jamie,' Mrs Murray told Thea. 'My greatest sorrow is that I can't see him as often as I would like.'

'It's only natural,' Martha broke in. 'You've always been fond of children. Remember that young woman you once took in? You wouldn't hear of turning her out, not even when you knew she was expecting. And when the baby came, you gave it all the love you gave your own.'

As Thea dived to hide her paling face by filling up the teapot again, Mrs Murray smiled sadly. 'She was such an adorable baby, and I loved her. More so, I think, because I was never blessed with a daughter of my own.'

'How she used to trail after Mr Logan!'

'Well, he had a lot of patience with her,' Mrs Murray paused reflectively. 'It used to surprise me a lot as he's never been what I call a terribly patient person, but he always had a lot with children and small animals. Small, helpless things.' Unconsciously her eyes went to Thea, who didn't see her quick glance. 'I don't think he's changed as much as we've thought, Martha.'

Christmas Day passed so smoothly that Thea couldn't quite believe it. Everyone helped, with Mrs Murray insisting on taking charge in the kitchen and relegating Thea firmly to the role of assistant. Thea didn't mind. After her first surprise, she found she actually enjoyed having the responsibility of such an important occasion taken out of her hands. She was learning, and fast, but it was nice to be able to relax. Sometimes, for all she was astonished at the pleasure she found in her work, her lack of experience could make her feel oddly tense.

After breakfast she went to her room and brought down her load of presents, trying to do this as unobtrusively as possible. Mrs Logan had already given Jamie her present so Thea didn't feel she would be stealing anyone's limelight.

Jamie, predictably, was delighted with the radio and train set which Thea had bought for him and couldn't decide which to concentrate on first. His excitement was such that she resolved to remind him, at the first opportunity, not to forget the less exciting books and puzzles his grandmother had produced.

Thea thought Logan was momentarily angry that what she had given Jamie far outshone anything else he got, but she couldn't be sure. Fleetingly his green eyes smouldered and then his expression was blank again. Lifting her chin a little, Thea stopped looking at him, the knowledge that she would soon be gone filling her with a kind of reckless bravado. Martha was so pleased with her present she seemed almost overcome, while Mrs Murray accepted her chocolates gracefully, with a warm smile. Logan, however, merely glanced briefly at his socks, never saying a word.

He distributed his presents himself, surprisingly expensive ones, or so they appeared to be to Thea, if not as well chosen as her own. There was nothing for herself, which made her face fall and her expectant flush fade. Mrs Murray, having turned to speak to Jamie, didn't notice Thea moving unhappily away, trying to hide the sudden tears in her eyes. Murmuring a hurried excuse, she went out, only to have Logan catch her up in the hall.

'Thea!'

Still unable to look at him, she paused. 'I've a lot to do, Logan.'

'Not right at this moment, surely?'

She bent her head, not prepared for the hands which swung her around, the fingers which tilted her chin up to meet narrowed dark eyes. 'I've hurt you, haven't I?'

'A little.' She had the honesty of extreme hopelessness.

He muttered something she didn't catch, under his breath. 'You're an amazing young person, Thea Andrews! You've been wrong all along, yet you manage to make me feel a brute, and I don't like it.' He went on regarding her intently, his jaw tightening when, uncharacteristically, she made no attempt to defend herself. 'Thea, child, I do realise you're alone in the world, and I suppose you thought that today was going to be nice and easy. Presents all round, sweet words and goodwill towards and from everybody. Well, you'd better get it into that pretty but very foolish head of yours that, a long time ago, I left that all behind me.'

'I'm sorry,' she whispered hoarsely, in total anguish, the eyes she lifted to him swimming now, her tender young mouth trembling. 'I deserved that, I know I've been utterly foolish ...'

Something about her, with her defences down, seemed to get him in spite of himself. 'Thea—come here.'

She was aware that he was more than just mildly exasperated as he drew her gently into his arms, holding her close, comforting her as he might Jamie. But a trembling pink mouth and rain-washed grey eyes must have been more than he had bargained for, for with a muffled exclamation he dropped his mouth to hers, stilling the trembling, opening it to wonder.

Through a daze, some words of his kept coming back. 'It's not enough. Not nearly enough!'

'Logan,' she didn't try to hide the stardust in her eyes as he raised his head, nor to remove her hand which had strayed against his cheek, 'that's the nicest present ...'

'Logan ...!' Thea jumped, wrenching herself from his arms as his mother's voice broke in uncertainly.

Turning slowly and deliberately, he shielded Thea with his big body. 'Yes, Mother?'

Clearly startled by what she had apparently seen, Mrs Murray was as intimidated as Thea often was when Logan used that particular tone, holding, as it did, a subtle warning that the subject under contemplation was not to be pursued. Her puzzled glance lingering on Thea, Mrs Murray, with obvious reluctance, gave in. Hesitantly, she said, 'I thought I'd just give Ingrid a ring. I know she spends Christmas with her people, but I did feel I should wish her well.'

'Give her my regards,' Logan replied evenly, with nothing in his manner to betray if he was pleased by the interruption or otherwise. His hand snaked out to grasp Thea's. 'Thea and I will return to the kitchen and keep Jamie company until you finish.'

That evening Thea wore her long pink dress and brushed her long fair hair until it shone. She put on a soft pink lipstick and tripped downstairs in silver sandals on curiously light feet, but though both Mrs Murray and Martha told her she looked lovely, Logan said not a word and made no attempt to come near her again. The day, which had proved such a success, and still was as the drawing-room curtains were drawn against the falling snow and the huge log fire made flickering reflections on tired but contented faces, suddenly palled for Thea, although she wasn't sure why.

The day after Boxing Day, McLean rang again. This time Thea answered the call as Logan was out and Mrs Murray had joined Jamie for a walk around the loch. She didn't know Ian McLean, but he sounded very nice and she couldn't bring herself to refuse to speak to him. He apologised for the accident in the village and hoped she had recovered. He had wanted to call and see her but Logan had told him he wouldn't be welcome.

After waiting in vain for the comment Thea dared not make about this, he asked if she would accompany Logan and his mother to the dance which his parents were giving the next night. While Thea tried with some confusion to decide what kind of relationship the two men must share, he added, 'Didn't Logan pass on my invitation?'

She had to ask Logan about it, she couldn't wait until he came home from the fields. Why hadn't Logan mentioned this invitation? He couldn't know she was a good dancer and loved to dance, but he might have guessed, if only because she was young, that she enjoyed an evening out occasionally. He certainly made it plain enough that he would be pleased to see the last of her, himself, so why should he mind if another man sought her company?

The snow which had fallen over Christmas lay white and hard under a frosty sky, turning the moors and the mountains and lochs into stretches of sparkling beauty. The snow was hard on stock. Duncan, who had spent Christmas Day with them at Drumlarig, had explained to Thea a little of the hardship it caused. She knew Logan was hoping the winter wouldn't be a severe one, but Duncan had said that the signs weren't good. Thea wondered, as her breath floated like white mist on the late afternoon air, how anything so beautiful to look at as snow could be quite lethal in places like this.

She found Logan at last, attending to a herd of cattle on the moors some distance away. Rather breathlessly, for she had walked further than she had intended, she stopped beside him. As she approached and he saw her, he watched enigmatically but silently.

'Mr McLean rang again,' Thea spoke to his raised eyebrows. 'He's asked me to go to the party his parents are giving tomorrow evening.'

'And he asked why I hadn't passed on his previous invitation?' Logan said dryly, quite able to observe this from Thea's flushed face and accusing eyes.

'You could have said something,' she reproached him, staring at him, already her grievances and Ian McLean fading as she rapidly forgot everything but Logan. He dominated her so that it was difficult to think of anyone else. Always, when she least expected it, it happened, giving the sensation of being swept by a flood tide. Despising such weakness in herself, she faltered, 'It's Christmas, after all.'

'Someone has to stay and look after Jamie,' he rejoined mildly, refusing to get annoyed.

A frown creased Thea's brow as she placed her feet more firmly on the slippery snow. She hadn't thought of that. She didn't truthfully mind so much about the party, but she would have enjoyed going out with Logan. It would have been something to remember. 'Maybe your brother's wife would come and stay with him?' she suggested recklessly.

'Ingrid's going to the dance,' he told Thea curtly. 'I promised to pick her up.'

Unconsciously, Thea's eyes widened despairingly on Logan's hard face, as pictures danced through her mind. Logan, taking a triumphant Ingrid to the ball, his hand, those long, lean fingers which Thea had known herself, fast on Ingrid's arm. They would dance together and he would hold her close, because Murray of Drumlarig was no hermit, much as he might pretend to be one. All this while Thea Andrews stayed at home. Why, even Cinderella had had a better deal than that! At least she had been given a chance to enjoy herself before being relegated to the kitchen sink!

Clenching her frozen hands, her eyes sparkled with anger. 'I hate you!' she snapped, hurt tearing at her because she loved him so. 'I suppose it wouldn't suit you to be seen at a social gathering with your housekeeper!'

'You little fool!' he snapped straight back, his eyes brilliant with anger. 'Would you really enjoy the elegantly raised eyebrows, the loaded looks, the conjecture? It might have been all right if you'd been old and fat, but you happen to be far too young and beautiful.'

It couldn't be because of that. Her breathing shallow, Thea thought she knew the truth. He wouldn't want anyone to get any odd ideas about his relationship with his housekeeper, not with Ingrid around. Hadn't Ingrid hinted that Logan might ask her to be his second wife? He was going to need someone, and hadn't he openly confessed he was tired of housekeepers who came and never stayed?

'You'll be leaving in a day or two, after my mother goes,' she heard him reminding her, 'so why start a lot of silly speculation?'

Of course he was right. 'No,' she muttered, her voice unsteady, 'it wouldn't be worth it, would it?' She twisted to leave him, to go home. Logan was so tall, he towered above her, swamping her, and she felt miserable. She seemed to have made a fool of herself.

'Wait until I finish haying these cattle,' he still looked at her keenly, 'then you can ride on the tractor with me. I won't be long.'

She waited, watching as he cut open the bales of hay with a knife before tedding it out into upright feeders, through which the cattle could eat the fodder without trampling it into the ground. She had been living in a

fool's paradise, she supposed, seeing herself floating round
a ballroom in Logan's arms. And while she wouldn't have
minded so much about what people might have said, she
would hate to embarrass Logan's mother.

He finished his task and came back to her. 'Would you
like to sit on the trailer? You might find it more comfortable.'

'More appropriate, I think you mean?' Feeling so bitter
she was prepared to exaggerate everything, she stared at
him defiantly. It would never do for the master of Drumlarig to be seen with his housekeeper in the cab of his
tractor, riding with him there, as Jamie often did.

'Don't get too sensitive, Thea,' he warned sardonically. 'The lowering of one's pride a little isn't a great price
to pay for the rewards that might follow. With your reputa-
tion unsmirched—who knows, McLean might even ask
you out again, on a more private occasion.'

'I don't need you preaching to me, Logan,' she said
stiffly, taking no comfort from his dryly given advice. She
felt only frightened when he talked like this. It emphasised,
as he appeared to be doing quite frequently, that he had
no particular interest in her himself. 'I have no real wish
to go anywhere with Mr McLean, and I don't think I
have anything to thank him for. I just thought it was kind
of him to ask me to his party, or ball, or whatever it is,
but I'll ring and tell him I'm not coming, as soon as I get
home.'

Logan's mouth relaxed slightly, but he didn't smile,
'Leave it,' he cautioned abruptly. 'Better that we simply
turn up without you.'

Feeling she had to make a stand somewhere, Thea protested stubbornly, 'I was taught that it's good manners to
let people know.'

'Sometimes,' he agreed, 'but what sort of explanation
would you give in this case?'

Was he never wrong? Meeting his level gaze, her own

reflected frustration, seeing in his hard eyes a challenge she didn't know how to handle.

'Come on,' he said quietly, 'things are seldom as bad as they seem. Cheer up!'

Because she couldn't be sure her love for him didn't show, she said sharply, 'I don't have to listen about rainbows and silver linings!'

'You don't believe in them?'

'Not very often.'

He laughed. 'Then I'll have to prove to you that they do exist, and should exist, for someone as young as you.'

'You'll have no time,' she reminded him. 'I'll be leaving soon.'

'True enough,' he agreed curtly, his glint of mocking amusement fading as, to her surprise, he lifted her bodily and impatiently, placing her firmly on the trailer. So that all she could think of, on the way back to the standing, was the ruthless strength of his arms.

When he drew up inside one of the huge covered yards he had built, she jumped off the trailer at once, but almost as if he had anticipated her intentions, Logan was there before she could run away.

There was a flicker in the depth of the dark eyes which sombrely regarded her flushed face. She felt the vibrations of it coming towards her, as though he generated some kind of unnerving force, a force which threatened to crush all her defences.

'Thea,' he said as she quivered, 'I haven't thanked you properly yet for making our Christmas so pleasant. In Scotland we don't always make a lot of Christmas, but this year I really enjoyed it.'

'I'm glad.'

He placed an apparently idle hand against the side of the trailer, so she couldn't leave without obviously ducking around him, 'I didn't explain, either, why I was angry when you produced your presents.'

At least he didn't pretend he hadn't been! 'It doesn't matter now ...'

Lazily he lifted his free hand to remove a piece of straw from her hair, making her heart beat too quickly. It was the second time within the past hour that he had done something to disconcert her. If she hadn't known better she might have thought he was considering his next words.

'I'm not without intelligence, Thea. At a rough calculation, I could almost guess how much you had spent.'

'It—it was my own money.'

'I wasn't suggesting you stole it,' he ran an impatient hand over his own hair now, thrusting it back, 'but I understood you were down to practically your last penny.'

'Not quite,' she muttered, not looking at him, but unable to stop the faint flush that came to her cheeks. 'I—I earned a little in London, before I came here.'

'I won't ask how.'

Blankly her eyes flew to his, colliding head-on with the cold condemnation in his, as they flicked darkly over her slender, sensuous body. She felt her limbs tingle, her pulse race, as though he had actually touched her. She had wanted his approval, but it couldn't have been clearer what he was thinking. Dismayed, she jerked back, coming painfully up against the side of the trailer, for she wore nothing but a thin sweater, that didn't protect her.

'You don't believe ...!' she gasped.

His smile was cynical, as he lifted cool eyes. 'With strangers I keep an open mind. You're a very attractive girl.'

While nothing had been actually put in words, they both knew what was under discussion. Thea closed her eyes tightly for a second, to prevent them filling with tears. 'I don't think I'll ever forgive you!'

Logan didn't appear stricken. His mouth quirked, if grimly, as if he derisively surveyed his own foolishness. Lightly his fingers touched her cheek. 'You have the most amazing skin. It's smooth and satiny, like the petals of an exotic flower. The colour comes and goes, especially when you're annoyed with me. Have you ever been in love?'

The unexpectedness of his question startled her. It startled her even more, when she tried so hard to defy him, to hear herself answering with tremulous weakness, 'No, I've never been in love before.'

His perception, as always, was rapier-sharp. 'Was that last word really necessary? Did I merely imagine a brief hesitation?'

'No!' she cried, too vehemently, not liking the feeling that she was in danger of losing control over her own responses. Helplessly, her eyes fell on the strong column of his throat, which the open neck of his shirt laid bare. A pulse beat there heavily; she knew a sudden, urgent desire to lay her lips against it. Alarmed, she took a grip of herself, praying she could keep her head. Instinctively she felt Logan was punishing her for something she didn't quite understand, and she must continue to fight him. 'No!' she said again, making a greater effort to speak casually. 'Besides, you wouldn't believe I was old enough to be in love.'

'I might take some persuading that you're old enough to know your own mind,' he replied tightly.

Lightly she shrugged, as though not prepared to argue. Her eyes fell to the leather belt that fastened his trousers to the muscled leanness of his waist. If she looked at him and he was able to gauge the depth of her feelings, it might be more embarrassing for herself than for him.

When she made no reply, he straightened, his arms falling to his sides with a taut sigh. 'I won't say anything more about the presents you bought, Thea. Obviously you went to a lot of trouble over them and I'm sorry if I spoiled some of your pleasure, but don't do it again.'

'As I'm leaving, I won't have a chance, will I?' she retorted dully, walking away from him.

Jamie ran from the house as she approached it, coming to look for her. 'We've had a great walk, Granny and I,' he told Thea happily. 'She says I may go to Edinburgh and stay with her for a few days, if I'd like to. She thinks I'm old enough now to be able to appreciate everything.' He paused, gazing at Thea earnestly. 'The castle and all that, you know. She also thinks that if I'm to go to boarding school next year, a few small breaks beforehand will be good for me.'

Boarding school! Thea's heart sank. She knew all about that. Jamie was so young, but then she wouldn't be here. So there was no need to wonder how she would manage to put on a brave face when it was time for him to go.

Trying to imitate his happy smile, she looked at him. 'There's a lot of sense in what your grandmother says, darling, and I know she'd love to see more of you.'

'As long as you'll be here when I come home,' he said, unable to keep the uncertainty from his voice.

'Oh, come on!' she laughed, not daring to confess she wouldn't be, and trying to hide her unhappiness by grabbing his hand and pulling him teasingly indoors.

Neither of them noticed Logan standing behind them, so they didn't see the dark expression on his face.

CHAPTER EIGHT

THE following evening Thea helped Mrs Murray to get ready for the ball. Mrs Murray was so excited she kept dropping and mislaying things.

'I should never have managed without you, Thea, I'm sure. I do wish you'd been coming. I told Logan that no one would mind, but he says it isn't that. It seems he wants you to stay with Jamie. I do wish I'd thought of it sooner—we could have got someone reliable from the village to come in. There are still plenty who would be only too willing to oblige a Murray.'

'Stop worrying,' Thea laughed, pretending amusement, anything to convince Mrs Murray she didn't really mind about missing the ball. 'I didn't really want to go, and Jamie might be better with me. Logan (she felt ashamed that she had stopped trying to remember to call him Mr Murray, in front of his mother) is taking your daughter-in-law and if he knows Jamie's all right he'll be able to relax completely.'

'Yes.' Mrs Murray paused, then hurried on, 'I do know that Ingrid's coming, of course. Logan does work hard, doesn't he, dear? You know, when my eldest son died I prayed that Drumlarig could be saved for the family, but, to be quite truthful, I never dreamed Logan would manage it. When he did I thought my prayers had been answered, but I've often wondered since if I realised exactly what I was praying for. He's had such a struggle that sometimes I feel guilty about it.'

Thea, busily tidying the bedroom now that Mrs Murray was almost ready, didn't look up, but her voice sounded slightly unsteady. 'He seems to be making a success of it.'

'Yes,' Mrs Murray sighed, 'and I expect it will be better in a year or two. He never tells me very much.'

'Doesn't he?' Mrs Murray was so nice and understanding that Thea thought she would be very easy to confide in.

'We've been apart too long, I'm afraid.' Thea noticed Mrs Murray staring at her own reflection in the mirror, as if she didn't really see it, 'After my husband died and James took over, Logan left his university and went abroad. James and Ingrid were married and I went to live in Edinburgh with my youngest son. I haven't seen much of Logan since then. He needs a wife, not a mother, Thea,' she smiled wryly, 'but I hope that if he marries again he'll find more happiness with his second wife than he did with his first. Kay and he were never suited.'

Kay? Thea never forgot how Logan had spoken of her when he was delirious. Why had his marriage to her been unhappy? It was the impression she had had from Martha and his mother, from Logan himself. It didn't seem possible that they could all be mistaken.

She and Jamie, with Martha standing in the background, saw Logan and Mrs Murray off. Logan looked so splendid in his dress kilt and full regalia that Thea's breath caught in her throat. He put his mother in the car while Jamie returned to the warmth of the drawing room, but as Thea began to close the front door he came back to her.

Lightly he touched her hair, prodding his knuckles under her chin, his eyes glinting down on her enigmatically. To her utter astonishment he said, his voice low and slightly husky, 'If it hadn't been for my mother's sake I shouldn't have gone. I would have stayed at home with you and Jamie.'

The morning after the ball, Martha commented that it was Thea who looked as though she had been out all night.

Logan, lifting his head, glanced at Thea sharply but

didn't say anything. She believed he hadn't been to bed himself but simply changed his clothes when he had come in and gone straight out again to feed the stock.

Thea, who had slept badly, didn't reply to Martha's taunt either; she was used to them by now. Instead, after asking Logan politely if he had enjoyed the ball and receiving a brief reply to say he had, she got on with her work, putting out of her mind a certain expression which she had thought she had caught in his eyes, as he had left her, the previous evening.

A day later Mrs Murray left. Logan took both Jamie and Thea to Fort William to see her off. Thea felt almost tearful as she said goodbye. There was so much she had wanted to speak to Mrs Murray about, and she wasn't sure if she would ever see her again.

Leaving Logan and Jamie to say their own goodbyes, and to see Mrs Murray comfortably seated on the train, she slipped into the booking office to enquire about the best connections for London. Logan didn't ask what she had been doing, when she joined him again, and she didn't offer any explanation. She guessed he knew what she had been doing and approved, for he smiled slightly as he nodded briefly at her.

After the train finally disappeared into the distance, and Jamie stopped waving, they left the station. The line was built along the shores of Loch Linnhe and today the greyness of the skies was reflected in the water. This looked as cold as Thea's heart felt, when she thought of the morning which must soon arrive when she, too, would be leaving on the train, just as Mrs Murray had done.

To her surprise, Logan took them out for lunch. He didn't consult them about it, he simply put them back in the car and drove them to the hotel. Just as if they were two children instead of one! Thea didn't know whether to feel vexed or pleased. The hotel he took them to was a little distance out of Fort William and strictly in the luxury class. They could have stayed in the town, he said, but he thought they would enjoy the drive.

As they sat down in the well appointed dining-room, she glanced about her anxiously. It was probably silly, but she was so used to thinking of Logan as poor that she worried when he spent anything. She wasn't really surprised to find him an expert on food and wine, not when she remembered he must have been fairly wealthy to have paid what he had for the Drumlarig estate. Idly she wondered how he had managed to accumulate such a lot of money. Then, because money, even to think of it, still depressed her, she turned to Jamie, happier to begin explaining things on the menu, which was partly written in French, to him. She wasn't conscious of Logan listening curiously.

The remainder of the week passed slowly, but it wasn't until after the New Year that Logan called her to the library. Jamie and Martha had gone to bed when the kitchen door opened and Logan walked in. Instinctively she realised why he wanted to see her.

'It's no use,' he immediately divined her apprehension, as their eyes met across the kitchen floor. 'It's not something that can be postponed for ever.'

Blindly she rose from her chair beside the stove, where she had just been considering what kind of biscuits he would like with his coffee, and followed him, as he turned abruptly and went out again. It wasn't until he was closing the library door behind her and motioning her to a chair that she found her voice.

Swallowing hard, she turned to him. 'Wouldn't it be better if I just packed up and went? I'm sure there can be nothing you want to discuss.'

'Maybe not,' his eyes were cool. 'It could be up to you. Sit down.'

She didn't want to sit down. She wanted to rush to her room, to prepare herself for the ordeal of having to leave

Drumlarig. Drumlarig and Jamie had become important to her, but Logan was even more so. To be put through torture was bad enough, without having to discuss the best ways of doing it!

She remained standing, even when she sensed his growing impatience. 'When you say it's up to me, do you mean that you'd like me to stay until you find someone else to look after Jamie?'

'No.' Taking no notice of her apparent determination to hold back, he drew her firmly towards the fire, pushing her gently down into a deep chair. From his great height he stood regarding her, noting she had gone extremely white. 'You were making enquiries about trains to London, I believe, when we saw my mother off?'

'I was checking, yes.' She stared at the fire.

'You don't really want to go, do you?'

She never knew when his statements were questions, requiring an answer. She waited until he repeated the last two words before shaking her head, 'No,' still she couldn't look at him, 'but you know that, Logan. We've been through it all before.'

'Not everything,' he amended grimly, without taking his eyes from her face. 'I couldn't have a housekeeper of your age, Thea, for reasons which, I agree, we've already gone into, but I could easily have a wife.'

'A wife?'

'Yes.'

'Oh, I see ...' For one startled moment her heart leapt, but thank heavens sanity returned in time. It was Ingrid, of course. He was informing her of his future plans so she wouldn't worry so much over Jamie. It was kind of him, knowing how much she cared for the boy. Cold with despair, Thea nodded. 'You've decided to marry your sister-in-law, Mrs Murray?'

'Now we are jumping to wild conclusions!' She shrank from the mockery in his voice. 'Whatever gave you that idea? No doubt she would do very well, but she doesn't altogether suit my purpose. For one thing, I suspect Jamie doesn't care for her.'

'Then ...?' as though drawn by the magnet of her own senses, Thea's eyes flew to his. 'Logan?' she whispered, 'please don't tease me.'

'I'm not trying to,' he retorted, his eyes shifting to the trembling unsteadiness of her mouth. 'It's you I have in mind, for a wife,' he said quietly. 'You don't think I'd discuss my marriage with anyone else but the woman concerned?'

'No ...?' Her eyes shimmered and she knew she must looked dazed. She was dazed, stunned. If she had felt shaken before, it was worse now. 'You'd be willing to marry me, for Jamie's sake?'

There was a little pause of foreboding while his mouth twisted cynically. 'Not entirely for his sake, my dear. You've proved yourself a very competent little house-keeper, I can't remember being so comfortable before. With you as my wife, a lot of my domestic troubles would be over.'

'But there's more to life than the domestic side of it,' she faltered. 'Would I be the right kind of wife for you in—in other ways?'

His eyes, as always fathomless, met her wholly frightened ones, assessing the uncertainty that was sending visible tremors through her slender young body. Calmly he said, 'You're young enough to mould to my ways. You couldn't,' he added cruelly, 'be worse than Kay.'

'Kay?' Thea stammered raggedly, having to ask. 'You loved her very much?'

'No,' his glance was cold on her hot cheeks, 'and you can believe me.'

Thea wanted to. Yet it didn't seem logical and the pain inside her wouldn't let her be content with such a brief reply. 'Then why did you marry her?' She shouldn't persist, but she couldn't seem to help it. 'You must have had a reason?'

'Not necessarily,' he rejoined flatly. 'It was something we just drifted into. Kay and I met abroad. We were both wandering—myself with some purpose, Kay with none. We were convenient to each other without the drawback of emotional ties. Then Jamie was on the way, something I never intended should happen, especially as we had begun to drift apart. Kay didn't want marriage, but I insisted, so I have only myself to blame. I was beginning to do well and saw myself with a stable home and family, but she didn't want any of these things. From the moment we married she changed and after Jamie was born she left us. She kept coming back, but just for one thing—money. Occasionally she even stayed a few weeks, but we never lived together again.'

Thea had been desperate to know such details, never dreaming that Logan's pain would only add intolerably to her own. His face was so hard it seemed to prove how painful this period of his life had been, but before she could tell him she had heard enough, he went on grimly, as if determined to punish her curiosity by making her listen to the whole of it.

'When I sold my assets abroad to buy Drumlarig, she was furious. She came here to look, to rage, to make demands financially which I couldn't meet. The last time she came she had her lover with her and they were both killed in an accident, driving back to London. I'd be a hypocrite if I said I wasn't relieved, but none of it seemed to make sense. It still doesn't. In a way I still blame myself.'

Thea swallowed a thick lump in her throat, 'I think perhaps you've done this too often. How old was—Kay?'

'The same age as myself.'

'So she must have been old enough to be at least partly responsible for her own destiny.'

'Perhaps.' His face was hard again, closed against any further sympathy.

Uncertainly, Thea stared at him. 'I'm sorry, anyway.'

'Don't be,' he replied curtly. 'I regard it merely as something you'd better know before you decide to marry me.' Again his voice hardened. 'If you decide to marry me it might help to know I'm not still mourning my former wife.'

Not finding this quite as comforting as he apparently intended it should be, Thea hesitated. If only it were as easy as that! Yes must be one of the simplest words in the English language, but it might also be one of the most dangerous. In this case it both tempted and repelled, leaving her wallowing in miserable confusion.

Something of this must have shown on her face. Logan eyed her grimly. 'If you had somewhere to go, Thea, even a good job to go to, I wouldn't be offering you marriage. Let's face it, you're practically destitute—and believe me, I know what that means. If I sent you away now, put you out, I'd feel as if I was doing it to Jamie.'

If he knew she had a home, and money, he wouldn't marry her. Confession on the end of her tongue, Thea actually bit it and just stopped herself from crying out as her nerves jumped with pain. She had a choice, maybe seconds to consider it. Either she must marry Logan and learn to live with this impression he had of her, or she must never see him again. She could stick to her former plan to give all her money to charity or find some means by which Logan and Drumlarig could benefit from it. This latter way appealed to her most, but whatever happened she knew that Logan must never hear about it.

She seemed to have no choice, but it was a decision she didn't make without pain. She didn't easily practice deception and following Logan's confession she had impulsively thought of the relief of making her own. Now she couldn't—it was as simple as that. Just as she couldn't possibly refuse to marry him. If Logan had loved her she might have felt able to tell him everything, but as things stood between them she couldn't afford to take any risks.

Unconsciously, as if some small, protesting part of her was still trying to put off the moment of complete commitment, Thea stammered, 'You wouldn't want a proper marriage, of course? It would be what's usually called a—a marriage of convenience.'

His mouth relaxed, but the smile he produced was grim rather than humorous. 'That's one thing I want you to consider seriously. If you do marry me, it won't be a marriage of convenience.'

Her cheeks uncomfortably flushed, Thea looked away from him. His last words had been so heavily accentuated she could never pretend to mistake his meaning. She wasn't as naïve as all that, but the thought of belonging to him completely was more than she could easily contemplate. Not immediately ... 'You don't love me,' she whispered hoarsely, 'so how can it be anything else?'

Showing a flicker of anger, he stared at her, as though fast losing patience with her wide-eyed pretence of innocence. 'A lot of marriages are reasonably successful without love.'

This didn't answer her question, but she dared not push him. 'I suppose so ...' Her voice faded uncertainly as she glanced blindly down at the hearthrug.

'Thea,' he sighed, his eyes on her downbent head, 'I can't promise the kind of marriage you seem to have in mind—friendship only, separate bedrooms?'

'But I've read about it.'

'It never works, not with two normally healthy people.'

'No?' She didn't know what else to say. He wasn't helping with his so down-to-earth attitude, and her mouth felt so dry it was difficult to speak at all. She tried to look at him, to voice some of her fears, but found it impossible.

His manner was crisp as he sat down beside her, his

piercing glance seeing her soft mouth trembling with uncertainty. 'Thea, I could promise a whole lot, but I'm a man and you're a woman, and there you have it. There is also some kind of magnetism between us which I think you're aware of.'

Her mind flinched from this, as her body shrank from his nearness. It was something they might have imagined. 'But we aren't animals,' she countered hollowly. 'You don't love me.'

'Because I feel this is an occasion when only complete frankness will do, it doesn't mean I'm an animal, my dear.'

Twice she had asked him, yet he hadn't denied he didn't love her. She loved him and would be willing to give him anything, if it would make him happy, but she could see now that some things might be far from easy to give when he didn't love her in return.

'What if you should fall in love with someone else?' she asked, feeling she would be unable to bear it.

'I won't,' he said thinly. 'I assure you I can be faithful, if you stick to the same rules yourself. And you'd better decide to,' he finished curtly, 'if you're going to marry me.'

Still she wasn't able to commit herself, although every part of her was urging her feverishly to do so. She gazed at him, her eyes reflecting something of her longing, the tensing of her body something of her apprehension.

'Thea!' he exclaimed tersely, taking hold of her hands and forcing her to look at him. 'I think you want to say yes, that you want to stay here with Jamie and me, and I can't understand all this hesitation. You've been around,' he continued brutally. 'This I can understand, and you don't have to feel compelled to act as if no man had ever touched you before.'

'I hate you!' she gasped, not taking into account that his opinion of her was one she had deliberately fostered herself.

'It might be better to calm down, rather than exhaust

yourself with imaginary emotions,' he retorted coldly. 'Do you really think I'd have either time or patience to take on an innocent young girl? I want a woman who'll be willing to give me what I want, with no fuss.'

Covered by his large ones, Thea felt her hands clench. She would never dare tell him that all her experience amounted to was a few chaste kisses.

Inexorably, when her face went white, he went on, 'I'll make you a promise, Thea. If you keep your side of the bargain, you won't ever need to walk the roads looking for a home again.'

Weakness invaded Thea's limbs, confusing her ability to think. She knew only an urgent longing, a sudden illogical desire to lay her head against Logan Murray's broad shoulders and give herself up to the remembered excitement of his arms. And their promise of a haven.

Her pale cheeks flushed scarlet as she managed to restrain herself. 'What you're trying to say,' she accused jerkily, 'is that you want someone to go to bed with, to provide you with more children and look after your house, so you can forget about all three?'

For a moment his eyes flickered, then he said dryly, 'It sounds worse spelt out, but you seem to have the general idea. I'll just stress that I'm not desperate. If it hadn't been for Jamie I doubt if I would have mentioned marriage at all. And I'm not using force, it's entirely up to you.'

'All right, I accept.' Briefly she closed her eyes, unable to resist her own clamorous heart; unable to bear the thought of not seeing him again.

The tightening grip on her hands as he drew her slowly to her feet was the only contact, but she felt her head reel. She tried to look at him but found it difficult as her heart lurched crazily. His face, with its high cheekbones and straight nose, seemed to be hovering hazily above her. She hadn't realised his mouth was so sensual yet finely moulded, self-willed. When he bent down, brushing his lips lightly

across hers, as though to seal their bargain, she closed her
eyes, fighting the urge to fling her arms around his neck
and drag him to her. Even so, she could feel herself beginning to spin, warning her of a whirlpool in which she might
eventually drown.

His voice came from a great distance. 'You're absolutely
sure you know what you're letting yourself in for? I
won't allow you to change your mind, once you walk out of
here.'

'I won't,' her throat ached with suppressed emotion, but
she made herself go on. 'I've given you my promise and I
don't cheat.' Suddenly she stopped, wondering why each
word should rear up and mock her. 'I don't cheat,' she
muttered, feeling like someone drunk on their own deceit.

The sensation which suddenly flowed between them
made her shiver. His touch released such a torrent of
emotion it made her weak. She was no stranger to his
breath on her face, and as she felt it quicken roughly her
own accelerated to match it.

Nervously alarmed, she stepped back, but, as if impatient of her reactions, he held her tighter. 'If you shrink
like this now, you'd perhaps be wiser to think again?'

If only his voice had held one softer note! 'Could I
have time?' Her courage rapidly disappearing, her great
eyes implored him more beseechingly than she knew.

'How much? Six months? And after that another six?'
he jeered cynically. 'You aren't in a position to play for
time, child. It has to be either yes or no, and now!'

Of course it had to be yes. There was no way she could
bring herself to refuse him. Silently she might argue that
with a little more will-power she might do so, but Logan
and Jamie, with Drumlarig thrown in, were too powerful a combination to resist. All she ever wanted was here,
but most important, the two people she cared for most in
the world. Here was a future to start dreaming of, to be
part of, to help to shape. Logan had said he would mould

her, but she was wise enough to know that a wife's influence counted for a lot. In this instance, Thea was suddenly determined that hers would help to make Logan a new man, a man who would lose the bitterness from his face and learn to smile again without cynicism. And maybe one day, if she tried hard enough to please him, he might begin to love her.

Suddenly the future didn't appear black any more. Thea's look of apprehension was banished by a smile—a tentative one, to be sure, but one which lit up the gentle angles of her face, accentuating all her young, fresh beauty. 'Yes,' she said clearly, lifting her chin and, despite her racing pulse, able to look him clearly in the eye. 'Yes, I'm quite sure I want to marry you, Logan, if you really want me to.'

A week later they were married in Edinburgh and after the ceremony left for London, for the weekend. Jamie, quite jubilant with delight at such a turn of events, was to stay in Edinburgh with his grandmother until they returned to pick him up on the Sunday evening.

Mrs Murray had been delighted when Logan rang to tell her that Thea and he were to be married. She had frankly confessed that she had prayed this might happen, for all their sakes. On arriving in Edinburgh Thea had been almost moved to tears by the welcome she received. It seemed to her like a miracle that she was so warmly accepted, and once more part of a close family circle.

Thea had wanted to go straight back to Drumlarig, but Logan had insisted it would be easier if they had a few days in London first. While she couldn't argue about this, she wasn't at all keen to go to London, as it seemed to be the centre of all her guilt. To refuse, however, might only draw Logan's attention to it. She could only protest feebly that it might be nicer to go elsewhere, but when he told her quietly that he had some business there which he must attend to, she had said no more. What, after all,

could happen? Even the chances of seeing someone she
knew were so remote as to be scarcely worth considering.
If they did bump into someone, no one, Thea felt sure,
would have the nerve to start talking of his wife's money
to a brand new bridegroom. Certainly not to a man like
Logan Murray.

When they took a taxi from the airport to one of the
city's largest, most luxurious hotels, she thought she
understood why Logan had made her buy some smart
new clothes in Edinburgh. Not a lot, but they included
two evening dresses, which she could see now she was
going to need. With the knowledge of all the smart clothes
hanging in her London flat, it had taken a great deal of
self-control to stay silent about them. She had had to
positively force herself to allow Logan to buy those she
was now wearing. Not once had he left her side and given
her the chance of paying for them herself. The money, she
felt unhappily, might have been better spent on the estate,
and she was terribly apprehensive as to what he would
say if he ever found out about her legacy.

At Edinburgh, in the cathedral, she had felt so proud
of him. He had turned slowly to watch her walking hesitantly towards him, and when she reached his side he had
taken her hand, holding it tightly in his until her first,
trembling nervousness had passed. As she had regained a
little composure she had been almost startled by a fleeting
tenderness in his eyes. She had known she looked surprisingly lovely in the white dress, a present from Mrs
Murray which had also been bought in a great hurry, but
she had never guessed that the first sight of her would
affect Logan so strangely. His jaw had gone tight and
there had been a rather frightening whiteness about his
mouth, together with a leaping flame in his eyes. But when
she had looked again, it had been gone and there had only
been the momentary tenderness which, although reassuring, was vaguely disappointing.

Glancing at him, as they were shown to their suite, she felt proud to be seen with him. He was so good-looking in his well cut grey lounge suit. She saw his hair so dark as to be almost black and his eyes which were often expressionless but always alert. Beneath his square brow and straight nose was a very firm mouth and chin. If only he had loved her this could have been a perfect day. Already her new mother-in-law liked her and Jamie made no secret that he was ready to adore her, but this could never make up wholly for Logan's lack of affection. Thea had hopes of winning his love. Sharing his bed might partly achieve this, but curiously she found herself shrinking nervously from such a final commitment. It was even difficult to think of when for him this would mean merely the gratification of his physical appetites.

'Like it?' she heard him ask formally when they were once more alone.

'Oh, yes.' Forcing an appreciative smile, she gazed about her, having been too absorbed with her immediate thoughts to concentrate on her surroundings. Her smile faded to a quick frown as she realised just how luxurious their rooms were. 'Logan, are you sure you can afford this? Honestly, I wouldn't have minded something not quite so—well, you know what I mean.'

His face darkened and belatedly she wished she had kept her mouth shut, but his reply, she was relieved to hear, belied his momentary anger. Carelessly he shrugged, 'As it's only until Sunday I think I can manage it.'

In the slightly brittle silence that followed, Thea wandered aimlessly to the dressing unit, nervous again at being so alone with him yet eager to make amends for her thoughtlessness. 'I didn't mean to sound ungrateful, Logan. Any girl would love this, naturally.'

'Usually women like luxury.'

'Now and again,' she agreed. He came up behind her and she added too quickly, 'London seems busy today.'

Slowly he placed his hands on her arms, drawing her around to face him. 'We needn't notice.'

Trying to smile at him again, she failed. Her face felt stiff. She wasn't sure what he meant, but her heart seemed to. Her pulse beat unsteadily as her eyes flew to his face. 'We won't have time to.'

He smiled sardonically. 'At least you'll have time to decide whether you like being married to me or not,' he drew her closer, 'Mrs Murray.' Unexpectedly he dropped his head and kissed her lightly, but made no further attempt to hold her. As she gazed up at him, he asked as he let her go, 'Would you mind if I grab the bathroom first, then you can have it as long as you like?'

He was only gone a short while. Thea scarcely had time to unpack her new bathrobe before he was back with only a towel wrapped around his waist. With a few confused words she hurriedly escaped, thankful that he would be dressed, ready for dinner, before she returned.

Hoping to give him ample opportunity, she soaked in her bath longer than she might otherwise have done. She thought, too, she might feel more relaxed, but it only gave her more time to think. London had disturbed her, taking away her new sense of security. If Logan insisted on his marital rights mightn't she be wiser to give in to him without a fight? If their relationship was cemented in this way he wouldn't find it so easy to get rid of her if he ever discovered how she had deceived him. Loving him as she did, she was convinced it would be no hardship to go on living with him, even if he came to hate her.

Feeling strengthened by her new resolutions, Thea dried herself on one of the beautiful pink towels provided. She had almost forgotten how nice really thick towels could be. After sprinkling her still damp limbs with a fragrant dusting powder, she wrapped her bathrobe tightly around her slender body and left the bathroom.

To her dismay she found Logan sitting on the edge of

the big double bed. He had discarded his towel for a short dressing-gown and was reading an evening paper. She wondered why he wasn't in the adjoining bedroom of the suite and failed to prevent herself from glancing at it pointedly.

'I'll get dressed,' she said quickly, averting her eyes from him, her cheeks regrettably pink.

'No hurry, is there?' he rejoined smoothly, putting aside his newspaper but making no effort to comply with her unspoken hint.

Thea, determined not to allow her churning thoughts to get out of control, passed a little too near to him and he idly grabbed hold of her. 'Come here, Thea,' he said softly.

When she instinctively resisted the pull of his hand, he was up on his feet in a moment. Still holding her, he stared down, to where her thin robe temptingly outlined her near perfect curves. His eyes darkened as his voice thickened slightly, 'Don't you realise just how beautiful you are? You make me feel impatient. And almost glad you've been around, so that you aren't going to be scared of me.'

But she did feel frightened, much as she tried not to. In the bathroom she had been stern with herself, refusing to allow her own shrinking reticence. She had known what she must do, what Logan would expect of her, yet her whole body seemed to scream in protest, either unwilling or unable to help her.

'Logan,' she murmured breathlessly, trying to laugh lightly, turning her face from his prolonged scrutiny, 'first things first. I'm hungry!'

'So am I,' he muttered indistinctly, the darkening passion in his eyes making her catch her breath. 'I want to give you all the time you feel you need, Thea, but you're so lovely you're making that almost impossible.'

'Please!' she entreated, but he appeared both deaf and blind to her pleading as he drew her gently closer, as he tilted her chin and his mouth came down to cover hers.

The feel of his mouth brought shivers of mindless ecstasy, but the fear in her mind kept her own mouth tightly closed against the warm insistence of his. She knew a strange urge to fight him; she might have done if something hadn't warned her in time. She had known what she was entering into; she had given a promise and she must keep it. She had never been truly honest with him and she mustn't add to her sins by trying to cheat him of something which was his by rights. Hadn't she married him? Wasn't she his wife? Besides, fully aware now of the warm feelings which rushed over her, she wasn't even sure if she wanted to cheat him any more.

'Logan,' she whispered, her lips parting as she forced her hands to his waist, then slid them, in apparent submission, around him.

CHAPTER NINE

As if that was all the encouragement he needed, Logan drew her tighter against his hard body, making her quickly aware of how she was arousing him. 'Don't fight me,' he said thickly, sensing her uncertainty. 'I didn't intend this to happen so soon, but it seems to be happening. You go to my head.'

Her lips trembled as they softened. She could feel herself dissolving, drowning, under the increasing urgency of his mouth. As he kissed her and his hands caressed her, fire seemed to crawl down her spine, filling her limbs with a great weakness and yearning. His eyes were pure green, passion leaping in their depth, and suddenly she was responding to him, fiercely. Helplessly she heard herself breathing his name, a world of longing in her voice, over and over again.

'I want you,' he groaned, his mouth against the warm hollow of her throat, 'I want you very much, Thea, you're driving me crazy!'

She wanted him too—she didn't want to hold anything back. She was afraid, yet her senses were heightened to a pitch of restless excitement. She was on fire and she could feel the heat of his body as he pressed over her. She strained towards him as he turned all her former vague longings into positive need, yet some part of her still held back.

'Relax, Thea,' his voice was husky as his mouth returned to hers, parting her lips hungrily, 'I'm not a stranger and I'm not playing games. I don't know how much longer I can stay sane. Drive me too far and I might hurt you.'

As he threw off his dressing-gown and crushed her to

him, her hands moved blindly over him. Now he seemed somewhere beyond words and she couldn't speak herself. Instinct swamped reason as a feverish passion cleaved her to him, paralysing her with desire. His relentless command over her left her shaking, but she could no longer hide the messages sent out by her yielding body. Logan didn't love her, but she loved him, which must make this partly right, somehow. Whatever the outcome, there was no way she could avoid complete surrender.

'Logan,' she moaned, 'Logan ...' Now she opened her lips under his, kissing him back, her hands sliding around his shoulders, her fingers digging into his bare flesh until she felt him shudder. Then her eyes closed as the desire between them surged. It came in waves, as his demands grew, tumbling her breathlessly until she was melting helplessly against him. He held her as though he would never let her go, taking her with him every inch of the way. She was rising and falling, drifting mindlessly, hearing his hoarse breathing yet deaf to what he was saying. She was aware of his tendrness, that he was trying to be gentle, until pleasure overwhelming him made him oblivious for minutes to her own startled cry of pain. Then, just as she wanted to cling to him again, she was free, as he rolled away from her.

The next morning, Thea woke early to watch him as he lay sleeping beside her. For a few moments she examined his face closely, making no move to disturb him. It wasn't that she didn't want to, suddenly conscious of her urgent love for him; she wanted to very much, but she felt almost ashamed of her own responsiveness to his strongly muscled body.

In an attempt to divert such wayward impulses, she turned her thoughts tremulously back to the previous evening. Logan had been strangely silent after making love to her. Glancing at him uncertainly from under wet lashes, she had seen that he had looked slightly stunned. Somehow, she had just wanted to fade quietly into the mattress, but as that wasn't possible she had struggled tearfully into her crumpled robe. Not for anything would she have confessed to feeling oddly cheated.

Suddenly his hand had come out to stop her, to her surprise very gently, although his eyes had again held traces of passion. 'Darling,' he said softly, 'I'm sorry. If only you'd told me, I'd have used more restraint. It's never so good for a girl the first time, but it will be better after this, I promise you.' His breathing steadying slightly, he had hesitated, his eyes on her full, sensuous mouth. 'Do you want to go down for dinner, or would you rather stay here with me?'

He had left her in no doubt as to what he would have preferred doing, but he hadn't protested when she had declared, perhaps too vehemently, that she was still hungry.

'Come on, then,' he had said curtly. Then, his eyes softening ruefully, he had kissed her tenderly before getting up off the bed to go to his wardrobe to seek a shirt. He had seemed as indifferent to his own state of undress as he was to the mixture of fascination and outrage in her eyes as she watched him. Such things, his broad back had informed her arrogantly, she would have to get used to.

They had gone down to dinner, but the mood hadn't been right. Logan had seemed curiously on edge, while Thea had been too aware of new sensations, if not fully comprehending, to relax. The meal had been superb, but she hadn't been conscious of what she was eating. She hadn't been able to stop looking at him, every now and again stealing little glances, wishing more, with every passing minute, to be back in his arms, longing now for his more intimate touch. Where, before, she had been frightened, she now wanted to be close to him, to know again the feeling of his heated lips running over her skin.

She found herself wishing she had complied with his

taut suggestion that they stayed in their rooms. If he had hurt her she quickly forgot it and was filled with a new, impatient eagerness. This she had tried to hide, but later, as they had danced on a dimly lit floor, it became very obvious that she was betraying herself.

'Thea,' he protested tersely, as she pressed more closely against him, her slight figure enticing, in a gown that showed quite a lot of it. Softly his voice lowered to a groan. 'Do you know what you're doing to me? I want you to come upstairs. No more putting off.'

And it had been as he had promised the second time. Very quickly he had made everything right for her, and then more slowly, throughout the night, he had taught her much about the art of loving. Sometimes he had been gentle, sometimes not, but he had not done anything to spoil her growing love for him. If he had loved her, too, she knew it would have been perfect.

Aware of being watched, he woke up, smiling at her lazily. Then the smile was gone from his eyes, to be replaced by a smoulder of passion, as he took in her pale langour, the warm invitation of her softly parted lips. Turning on his side, he leant over, covering her mouth with his own.

Some minutes later he murmured, 'Do you remember the first time I kissed you? You had a cold and felt very sorry for yourself.'

Reluctantly she opened clouded eyes. 'I remember, but you don't,' she heard herself replying.

'Say that again?' clearly believing she was muddled in her thinking, he bent to kiss her more thoroughly.

She stirred, trembling under his exploratory mouth and hands, doubtful if she would be wise to try to explain something he needn't know about. 'It was when I first arrived,' she tried to be light and brief, 'when you were delirious.'

He frowned, but not angrily. 'Do you mind telling me

exactly what happened? I didn't frighten you, did I?'

'You did a little, at the time,' she confessed, 'but you didn't hurt me. You just grabbed me and kissed me, more or less.'

'More or less?' Slowly he frowned again, yet sounded bemused. 'Do you know, I had vague recollections of something like that, but I thought I must have been dreaming. You're sure that was all, that I didn't hurt you?'

'Quite sure.' She couldn't possibly tell him the whole of it; how his embrace had excited her unbearably even then, how she had felt herself responding.

'I wonder,' he said remorsefully, 'that you didn't decide to leave there and then.'

'Perhaps,' her breathing became ragged as she moved nearer to him, 'it made me want to stay.'

'Shameless hussy!' he teased, but his voice deepened as his eyes went over her, taking in all her fresh, young morning beauty, her flawless skin, her shining, tumbled hair. Far from gently, his fingers pushed through it, to curve the back of her head. 'Do you know,' his voice was husky, 'I believe I'm glad.'

'You only believe you are?' she teased back, running an indignant hand over the mat of dark hairs on his broad chest. She hadn't dared do this before and wondered now at her own temerity. So quickly was being married to Logan changing her that when she was close to him like this she scarcely recognised herself.

With a half smothered groan he brought her to him, but the gasp she heard was her own startled breath as he kissed her. 'Stop asking silly questions,' he muttered against her mouth.

His eyes smouldered and he was no longer teasing. His breath quickened with hers as he laid her roughly back against the pillows and bent over her. Instantly all her young, feverish passion leapt to meet his, then there was nothing but the urgent clamour of her blood, as she responded to the strength and hardness of his body.

Later, temporarily at peace, they lay quietly. How soon, Thea thought drowsily, she was coming to feel almost a part of him. Like a satisfied but still hungry cat, she stretched her hands sensuously over him.

'Thea!' His arms tightened, then, with a groan of regret, he put her just as suddenly away from him. 'I'm forgetting. I have an appointment in, I should think, no more than an hour's time. If I do manage to make it, I'll need all my wits about me—not scattered all over the place, as they appear to be now.' He sounded stern, but a wry smile touched the corners of his mouth as he disentangled his legs from hers and swung himself out of bed.

'I remember you told me.' Thea had forgotten this was the reason why he had come to London. Now she wondered how this business could be urgent enough to interrupt their brief honeymoon. Yesterday she had been glad he had business to attend to. Today she felt curiously resentful, and it showed. Her grey eyes were stormy as she gazed at him.

Reading her betraying face, he said gently, 'I didn't know it would be like this, Thea, or I'd have tried to arrange things differently. This is too important to put off, however, and we still have this evening and tomorrow, the rest of our lives, I guess.'

He came back to where she sat hunched up, as if defensively against the world. A small smile played at the side of his mouth as he bent to kiss her. It was a gentle kiss, but as it appeared to alter his breathing he drew sharply back. 'Tonight I'll make up for my absence,' he promised hoarsely.

Although he hadn't said he loved her, because he obviously didn't, Thea felt a little happier, something about the expression in his eyes making her more confident about the future. Certainly Logan seemed to be changing. She could scarcely believe he was the same man whose air of grimness and cynicism had turned him almost into a stranger over the past week. Her response to his love-making she sensed had surprised him, as much as their mutual ability to please each other might have done. It could have been perfect, she thought sadly, if he had loved her, but perhaps she was asking too much. Any man might be pleased with a young bride who had proved, if unintentionally, that she was far from indifferent to him, but that wouldn't be enough to command his love.

Before he left, Logan pressed into her hands a wad of notes with strict instructions to go out and enjoy herself but not to wander far away. Before he went to keep his appointment, she shared a hurried breakfast with him, but he still refused to satisfy her curiosity as to where he was going. Who could he be seeing in London on a Saturday, she wondered, when most business premises must be closed for the weekend?

After hanging around the hotel until after lunch, when it was obvious he wasn't returning, she decided to take a walk to get some fresh air if nothing else. Being at Drumlarig must have spoiled her for cities, as she realised she was longing to be back there.

Logan had told her to spend what he had given her, but she couldn't bring herself to do this. There was nothing she particularly needed for herself, anyway. If he insisted she kept the money, she would put it aside and buy something for Drumlarig, later. In the meantime she contented herself with buying a few small presents to take home. She thought it wiser to pay for these from Logan's money, although she would rather have spent her own.

She could have gone and checked up on her flat. Perhaps she ought to have collected some of her clothes while she had the chance. Being a man, Logan would never notice a few additional items in her wardrobe. If he did, he would only suppose she had bought them with the money he had given her. Yet she couldn't bring herself to go near the flat. If she didn't visit it, she reasoned, it might be easier to go on pretending it didn't exist. Her conscience was already too troubled by the things she was keeping from Logan. Even now she dared not tell him about her inheritance. Particularly now that she was beginning to realise just how much she would suffer if he was to throw her out because of it.

For the next few hours she wandered rather aimlessly about the West End before returning to the hotel, but Logan didn't get in until well after six.

'I thought you were never coming!' she accused him, as he strode into the suite, looking extremely well.

'I did ring, darling, but you must still have been out.' Frowning, he touched her pale cheeks with gentle fingers. 'You didn't imagine I'd had an accident or something, did you?'

'Well, how was I to know?' Quickly she turned from him, her nerves taut. 'You've been gone a long time.'

'I know.' He ran a hand round the back of his neck rue-fully, yet he didn't look all that sorry.

Men! Stiffly Thea tried to hide her anger. They were all alike, capable of putting everything else from their minds when it came to business. All the same, she was slightly stunned by the depth of terror that had flooded her when she had started to think that something might have happened to him.

'Look, Thea,' he withdrew thoughtful eyes from her averted profile to glance reluctantly at the time, 'I'll have to hurry if we want to eat before the show.' He had booked seats at a famous West End theatre.

As he paused, his eyes appreciative of the lovely picture she made in the gold sequinned top she wore over a skirt composed of masses of scarlet chiffon, she was reduced to a half anxious perversity. 'You haven't said where you've been, or even kissed me. Do you like my dress?'

Having torn his eyes away from her, to begin removing

his jacket, he glanced at her again, ironically. 'Three questions, when there isn't really time to answer one. All right, woman! First, you look beautiful and I imagine you know it. Secondly, if I kissed you, I couldn't guarantee we'd get further than the bed. Lastly, as to where I've been. That I fully intend explaining later, after the show. After we come back here I have two things to tell you,' again he paused, allowing her to glimpse at the warm sensuality in his eyes as they went over her, 'two things which I'm hoping sincerely will please you—and make a great difference in our lives.'

'Why not until later?' she persisted curiously, her face suddenly flushed.

'Because they're so important we might not want to think of anything else.'

'Then we needn't go out at all.'

'We do.' He might have wavered, but his eyes were immediately steady on hers. 'You wanted to see this show and I think we have something to celebrate. And I want you to have something to remember until I can take you on a proper honeymoon, which might not be as long as you think. Just have a little more patience, darling, and you'll see, it will all come right.'

Thea was surprised to find just how much she did enjoy the show, until she realised that Logan constituted the greater part of her pleasure. Being with him like this was indeed heady magic. He might not love her, but he appeared to enjoy her company. Wistfully she found herself hoping that if he had any affection for her, it might grow.

During the interval he bought her a drink and they strolled in the foyer. 'You are enjoying yourself, aren't you?' Logan asked, a little tersely, as if it mattered to him.

Thea's smile was radiant, yet when it came to it she found she couldn't explain the true cause of her happiness. 'Yes,' she hedged, 'I'm glad we came.'

Flicking her a quick glance, his voice hardened. 'Perhaps you'll miss this sort of thing too much after we return to Scotland. After the novelty of living at Drumlarig wears off, it might be too quiet for you.'

Thinking immediately of his first wife, she hesitated, a shadow which Logan was not to know was because of Kay moving over her face. She didn't guess he had looked for an instant denial, nor did she notice his eyes grow cold as she searched over long for tactful words with which to convince him she wasn't at all like Kay.

'Let's get back to our seats,' he said abruptly. Uncertainly, she followed him, murmuring rather belatedly that she would never find Drumlarig too quiet, which even to her own ears sounded strangely unconvincing.

During the interval, while they stood in the foyer, Logan had nodded to several people, but there had been no one she had known. It was only as they were leaving that she was horrified to find Jerry Banks at her side. Feeling desperate, she would have walked straight past him, but his hand was on her elbow, clutching it, and without an obvious struggle she couldn't free herself. Logan paused politely. She could see he noticed her apprehension and wondered at it.

Too quickly she spoke. 'Oh, hello, Jerry. I'm sorry, but we're in a hurry. It's been—been nice seeing you ...'

Jerry's thin brows shot up. 'Hi, wait a minute, my darling, you can't brush off old Jerry like this! I know you haven't forgiven me for running out on you at St Moritz, but if you'd only waited!'

'Please, Jerry,' she shot an anguished, panic-stricken glance at Logan's frowning face, 'you know it wasn't like that.'

Charmingly, he went on, as if she had never spoken, 'I've been ringing your flat. I've been around there plenty of times, too, but you haven't been in. I even rang your solicitor, but all he would say was that you weren't at home, the silly old twit! I must say,' his smile turned into a sneer, 'it must be nice to be able to afford to go off when you like, where you like.'

'I'm married now, Jerry,' she exclaimed starkly. 'This is my husband.' She was so shocked she forgot to introduce them properly.

'Really, Thea my darling,' again Jerry's eyebrows rose mockingly, 'some men do fall on their feet!'

Terrified at the cold anger on Logan's face, she feared for one awful moment he was going to knock Jerry flat. 'Please, Logan,' white to the lips, she entreated him, 'let's go.'

For a few taut seconds she thought he was about to refuse, then suddenly, ignoring Jerry completely, he swept her outside. It had begun to rain and it was cold, but Thea wasn't conscious of the weather. The cold outside was nothing to what she felt in her heart, but, if her evening was ruined, she had a horrible premonition that there was worse to come.

Logan halted on the wet pavement, careless of the splashes on Thea's flimsy skirts. 'Where is this flat of yours?' he asked grimly, his eyes daring her to deny she had one, or to withhold its whereabouts.

It seemed to stun her how he was so ready to jump to the wrong conclusions. Already he was judging and condemning her on only sketchy facts. Logan stood looking at her as if she were a stranger. 'Are you going to believe everything that Jerry said?' she cried.

'It isn't true, then?'

Miserably she dropped her head, not able to wholly deny it. 'Some of it is,' she admitted, miserably.

'The address of your flat?' The black rage returned to his eyes at her halting confession, and his demands were no longer to be ignored.

Unhappily she mumbled an address close to Hyde Park, pretending not to hear his harshly drawn breath. 'Logan,' she begged feverishly, clutching his arm, trying to make him look at her, 'I can explain. We needn't go there.'

But already he was hailing a passing taxi, pushing her inside and giving terse instructions to the driver. Turning back to her only then, he asked, 'Do you have a key?'

'Yes.' She always carried one. Lately it had proved a constant reminder of her guilt.

They didn't speak again. Thea sat frozen with misery, knowing Logan wouldn't ever forgive her. Hadn't he been deceived before? Never again would he tolerate being put through the same kind of misery.

Inside the flat, his silence continued for several more minutes, during which time he explored the whole of it very thoroughly, as if he was an estate agent making a swift first inventory of every room. He even opened cupboards and drawers, running his eyes rapidly over Thea's extensive and obviously expensive wardrobe.

'So,' he exclaimed at last, his features cold with a freezing anger, 'this is the first place of deception to be unveiled. A West End flat, uniformed porter, no doubt a beautiful little sports model resting in one of the garages below. What more is there that I don't know about?'

'Logan ...'

'Thea!' he interjected furiously, with a brutal disregard for her ashen face, 'don't try stringing me along any further. I don't know why you decided to come to Drumlarig. You started a train of events which you must have known could only end in disaster, and the telling of more lies won't help.' He placed a hand at her throat, his grip tightening frighteningly. 'I want to know—everything!'

Her voice came hoarsely, as she stared at him helplessly. 'There's nothing much ...'

'Everything!'

This time she swayed, brushing her tumbled hair from off her hot forehead with shaking fingers. She didn't think he would actually hurt her, but she dared not continue defying him, if this was what she had been trying to do. Logan looked livid, his face grey, his eyes brilliant with anger. She felt stunned and lacerated by it, but she guessed it was no use trying to salvage their marriage by keeping all further knowledge of her money from him. The evidence of it here was too real to ignore, yet there was something she felt driven to speak of first.

Her eyes pleading for his forbearance, she asserted huskily, 'It wasn't as Jerry said, Logan. It was I who ran out on him. Not only him,' she floundered painfully. 'There was another girl with us, Pam, whom I'd always understood to be Jerry's sister, until I discovered in Switzerland that she wasn't his sister at all, and they were lovers. They were just using me to pay their bills.'

'And that bothered you so little that it drove you to the wilds of Scotland?' Logan rejoined with biting sarcasm. 'You obviously went to Switzerland contemplating an affair with him, if this other girl hadn't beaten you to it. Did you love him as much as all that?'

'Loved him ...?' In a daze of uncertainty, her mind not able to cope with the cold accusations he was throwing ruthlessly at her, she hesitated, searching frantically for the truth. Had she been just a little bit in love with Jerry? If she had been it had never gone further than her imagination. She knew it now for what it had been, a mild infatuation, nothing compared to what she felt for Logan.

She could see that he had mistaken her silence for damning evidence of guilt and she wasn't surprised when he went on slating her with words. 'Do you think I care what you did with other men? It's perfectly clear that you would have been willing to live with your friend Jerry if he'd asked you. So let's leave the obvious and have a little chat about this money of yours, shall we? The money you conveniently forgot to mention when you came to Drumlarig.'

A cold tremor of fear went through her, making her

'shrink from him. 'I don't want to talk about money, Logan. I just want to forget it.'

'How much do you have?' Unlike hers, his voice didn't rise but was all the more frightening because of that. 'Tell me!' he grated.

Trying to breathe evenly, she jerked her head back from his steely grip. Surprisingly he let her go and she could see he detested even to touch her. Helplessly driven, she named a figure. Hearing it without expression, he asked the question she had been dreading. 'Why didn't you tell me before we were married?'

'B-because,' she stammered, 'if you'd known about it you wouldn't have—you wouldn't have let me stay.'

'Does Drumlarig mean so much to you?'

Yes, she wanted to cry, but not nearly so much as you. Yet she found it impossible to tell a man who so obviously hated her that she loved him. Instead she whispered bleakly, 'You don't understand, Logan. After what happened with Jerry and Pam, I suddenly realised what an empty, useless thing money is on its own. Suddenly I didn't want any of it any more. I ask my solicitor to see about giving it all away, then I set off for Scotland.'

'Why Scotland and Drumlarig?'

'Why not?' Couldn't he stop firing questions at her, as though she were a criminal? The hate in his eyes was terrible to see, but still she didn't seem able to tell him about being born at Drumlarig. Pride wouldn't let her, this and her feverish desire to be accepted on her own merits. She didn't want his feelings influenced by some incident in the past, although she doubted if pride would provide much consolation after Logan was done with her.

He appeared to take her two brief words at face value. 'Anything for kicks, I suppose,' he commented cruelly. 'Everything you found at Drumlarig provided them didn't it?'

'I only wanted to help,' a note of pathetic eagerness crept into her voice. 'I still do.'

She might never have spoken. 'You found me in bed and while I was flat on my back you used your cunning to influence Jamie and Martha. And then, like a fool, I proposed to you, after swallowing everything you told me about being a poor little orphan.'

Numbly Thea protested, 'I did try to tell you, but it wasn't easy. I've been trying to tell you for weeks. In fact, I wanted Drumlarig to benefit from the money.'

Savagely he exclaimed, 'It never will, not from anything of yours. I have no use for your money, Thea. I expect it was merely a whim, but you'd better get this straight. I have no wish to be bought and subjected to a female dictatorship.'

'I'd never do that, Logan. You know I wouldn't!'

'You won't get the chance.'

Suddenly she was so frightened her legs gave way beneath her and she collapsed on the chair behind her. Why was he talking like this? As if their life together was over. Of course he was furious. Hadn't he the right to be? She ought to have told him about the money sooner, but surely he would forgive her? They had so much—and through the night he had made such passionate love to her. That in itself must mount for something. 'Logan,' she was conscious of feeling desperate, 'I'll promise never to touch a penny of that money again.'

'I'm afraid I don't want or trust your promises,' he retorted harshly. 'You've been deceiving me all along, haven't you? Nothing that a man with a clear head wouldn't have detected, of course. Grocery accounts for a fraction of what you'd actually spent. Clothes for Jamie, Christmas presents—need I go on?'

'Well,' she choked back a sob, 'you gave me so little for food we might have starved. Even the wage you offered——' she faltered, pausing unsteadily.

'Was nothing?' he countered, as she flushed unhappily. 'You wouldn't understand that that was a desperate attempt to attract the right kind of person.'

'Well, in my case it didn't, did it?' she flared, feeling driven.

'How true,' he sneered. 'However, that's all behind us now.'

A small wave of relief was immediately drowned in his next pitiless observation. 'You're very comfortable here. I certainly needn't have you on my conscience any longer.'

Bemused, Thea clasped the arms of her chair as she stared up at his baleful face. 'How do you mean? What do you intend doing with me, Logan? Please,' she entreated, as he made no reply, 'let's go back to the hotel. I don't want to stay here any longer.'

'I'm afraid you'll have to.' His narrowed, smouldering eyes went over her, as if he were seeing her for the last time. 'I'm going back to the hotel to pack, but alone. You're staying here.'

'You mean you're coming back here to join me?'

'No, I'm returning to Scotland—without you.'

As the full import of what he was saying hit her, she jumped to her feet, with the cry of a small, wounded animal. 'Logan! You can't leave me here, you can't!' When his only reply was to tighten his mouth grimly, her voice rose. 'Don't you understand? It would kill me, because I love you so!'

She hadn't meant to tell him, not until she was sure he loved her, but she couldn't keep it back. It had slipped out, but suddenly she didn't care that he knew. What comfort would she find in having kept her love secret if he left her?

He took not the slightest notice, his mouth might only have become a little grimmer. 'You only love yourself, Thea. I regret our marriage. I'm sorry I hadn't the sense to send you away weeks ago, but I'm certainly not lacking in that commodity now. Our marriage is over, my dear, fortunately before it's had time to do any more damage. We won't be seeing each other again.'

'No, Logan!' Tears were streaming down Thea's cheeks now, but she didn't realise. 'I love you—and there's Jamie. I love Drumlarig, too. We could all be so happy there. You see, I've never been used to cities and I've been lost in London. You can't leave me, Logan, I'd be lost now without you.'

But he was already striding through the door. 'Save your breath, Thea,' were his last words as he slammed it behind him.

When he had gone, Thea sank down on the floor. Laying her head against the edge of her chair, she sobbed. Logan couldn't mean the cruel things he had said. His anger had been terrible, but it couldn't stay at such a red-hot pitch for ever. He would soon be back.

Later, when she had more control of herself, doubts crept in. How could she be sure he would change his mind? He was quite capable of sticking to his opinions. She had had convincing proof of this at Drumlarig. Only a fool would believe he would never return there without her.

He had been gone for well over an hour before she gathered her stunned wits together and reached for the telephone. She must speak to him. She wanted to rush after him to the hotel, but the memory of his fury made her shudder. This way might be best as it was possible he would lock her out of the suite and refuse to speak to her.

She picked up the telephone, but there was no answer to her prolonged ringing, and when she enquired at Reception she was told that Mr Murray had checked out.

Afterwards, Thea thought she must have wept for a whole week. Seven bleak days that passed slowly and painfully.

The bitterness of total rejection hit her so hard she found it difficult to think straight. In the flat was tea, dried milk and biscuits. She lived on this diet for days until she began to feel so weak she was forced to go shopping for something more substantial. Even so, she found it difficult to eat anything, and while she had been away from the flat she had been terribly anxious for fear Logan rang while she was out.

It became increasingly clear that he didn't intend coming back, or getting in touch with her, and while her pride began to rebel, she knew she couldn't give up so easily. One evening she rang him at Drumlarig; late in the evening, when she was sure he would be in. When he answered she was dismayed to find she couldn't speak. Tears choked her throat and she had to swallow twice.

He gave his number again. 'Hello, who is it?'

She could hear the terseness in his voice. 'Logan,' she began tremulously, 'it's Thea. I must speak to you.'

'Sorry,' he snapped.

'If you'd only listen!' she gasped. 'I love you. I'm so miserable, so worried. Who's looking after you ...? Oh, please!'

'Goodbye!' he snapped again, replacing his receiver.

Immediately, blindly, she rang back. 'Logan, don't cut me off ...'

'Stop pestering me, then.' The line went dead, her hopes with it.

Unable to give up, she tried again the next night. The result was the same, and the subsequent hurt she endured was terrible.

The last attempt she made, a woman answered. Thea didn't recognise the voice, but she sounding obliging. She went to get Logan, but when she came back she said rather uncomfortably that he wasn't at home.

'Who are you?' Thea asked.

'Mr Murray's new housekeeper.'

Dully Thea rang off. So he had completely reorganised his life without her; he wouldn't want her any more. Until now she had hoped, but she could do that no longer. There was only suffering left, and already the intense pain of it was having a curious effect. After almost two weeks of weeping and thinking solely of Logan, she found her feelings consolidating, as if inside she was becoming a small deep-freeze. Sometimes she was sure if she stuck a pin into herself she wouldn't feel a thing, so numb was she becoming. It became so that she could actually think of Logan without breaking down, and while not certain what to make of it she was glad of the relief this brought.

One day she realised she looked a fright. Staring in the mirror, she saw lank hair, huge shadowed eyes and a body so thin as to appear to be fading away. With nothing but pride to rescue her from what she instinctively knew could develop into severe depression, she salvaged and used it as best as she could. Such wild ideas as had entered her head over the past weeks she put firmly aside. No good would come of rushing to Drumlarig and confronting Logan there. To see him and be again rejected would be more than she could bear, and she might only upset Jamie. Logan knew where she was. If he had forgiven and wanted her, he wouldn't have let anything stand in his way. He would have sought her out, and because he didn't, Thea knew their marriage was definitely over.

A week later her plans were almost complete. Later in the year she would go to university. She had done so well at school that this presented no problems. She thought of teaching; something to do with children as a possible career, for she was fond of them and now she would never have any of her own.

Until it was time to begin training, she decided to take a job in a hotel on the south coast and managed to get taken on by one that stayed open all the year round. With the completion of her plans she had given up her flat. The furniture wasn't her own and all her possessions she had packed in two suitcases. Having had a last look around, while waiting for a taxi, to ensure that everything was tidy, she was startled a little when the telephone rang.

Thinking it must be her solicitor, she frowned. What could he want? On her way to the station she had arranged to call and see him, to sign some papers. She hoped he didn't have a change of plan as she didn't want to have to come back again, all the way from Bournemouth.

But when she lifted the receiver it was Logan. 'Logan?' she whispered, feeling herself beginning to shake, with the terrible tremors which had made her almost ill since he had left her. 'Logan?'

'Thea? Is that you?'

'Yes.' Clearing her throat, she felt herself returning to ice again, able to say coolly, 'Yes, Logan, you've just caught me. I was going out.'

'Thea?' his voice was abrupt but urgent, as if this time he feared it was she who would ring off. 'I've something to ask you. Jamie has broken his leg.'

'Jamie—— Oh, no! Oh, the poor darling!' Compassion made her incoherent, bringing the tears that she thought she had conquered to her eyes. Brushing them away with her hand, she added unevenly, 'I'm sorry, Logan. How bad is he?'

There was a slight pause. 'He's asking for you.'

'Asking for me?'

'You don't have to be so surprised,' he said bitterly. 'You succeeded so well in making him fond of you while you were here.'

'I suppose you believe that was all part of my plan?' she replied steadily.

Clearly over the line came a harshly drawn breath, but she wasn't sure of the cause of it. Logan said, 'I'm not accusing you of anything, Thea. I'm thinking of Jamie.'

With a lightness she wouldn't have thought possible,

she answered, 'I'm afraid I can't do much from London. Would you like me to speak to him?'

'No,' Logan sounded hoarse, 'I want you to come here, if you will. I'd have come to London to ask you, but I can't leave Jamie.'

'What about your new housekeeper?'

He made no attempt to deny that he had one. 'She's quite good. Not as competent as you, but she fills a gap. At least there won't be a lot of work waiting, only Jamie.'

CHAPTER TEN

ONLY Jamie, Thea thought bleakly, as the train she was travelling on approached Fort William that same day. She had flown to Edinburgh and caught the train from there. Logan was meeting her at the station, but she didn't find the prospect at all frightening. He didn't mean anything to her now. She was beautifully numb all over and knew she would stay that way.

She did. Logan was standing in the station yard, searching the carriages anxiously with his eyes. The passengers disembarked, there weren't many at this time of year, and she noticed something like relief on his face as he spotted her. It was cold and snowing, and if her heart leapt it could only be the thought of seeing Jamie and Drumlarig again. For Logan she felt nothing.

Logan looked older, his face drawn, his skin grey. He must be terribly worried over Jamie.

'How are you?' He strode towards her, and suddenly she felt devoured by his eyes.

As she stepped back his eyes went over her and she felt all her new thinness exposed. Yet as he drew nearer his face was expressionless, the way she always remembered, watchful, guarded, implacably hard.

Close beside her he stopped, making no attempt to touch her except with his eyes. 'You came.' He didn't utter her name, nor did she say his.

'I promised I would.' She looked straight at him, marvelling that she could do so. The ice within her shivered and cracked a little but didn't shatter, 'I came for Jamie's sake,' she said very clearly.

'I'm grateful.' She might have been an obliging stranger,

Just for a moment did a flicker of some unrecognisable emotion cross Logan's face, then it was gone and he reached down to pick up her suitcase. 'I have the car outside, we'll soon be home.'

Again the ice inside her shivered, as though melting at the trace of warmth in his voice, but quickly she recovered. She even felt a faint stir of triumph that it was so, that being with him like this didn't affect her in the least. After the long days and nights she had spent weeping and longing for him, her reactions even startled herself.

She wasn't aware how white her face was, how very thin her young body had grown. She looked so vulnerable, Logan paused, his mouth tightening, his eyes tortured. 'Before we go, would you like a drink or a cup of tea?'

'Nothing, thank you. I'd rather we went straight to Drumlarig.'

'Just as you like.'

Glancing at him curiously, she sensed some kind of reluctance in him. Why? When it came to the crunch, was he discovering that he didn't want her back there, no matter what the circumstances? Or was it because of something else? Again, as they left Fort William, she dared another quick glance, wondering how, apart from his admitted good looks, she had ever found anything about him to love. How could a man as grim as Logan Murray have had such an attraction for a girl as young as herself? Thank goodness she had come to her senses in time!

Yet for all she found it easy to deny her love, she couldn't but be aware of the glad relief she felt at being back. Winter still clutched the countryside in its possessive arms. As yet there was little trace of blue in the sky, no buds on the trees, no green in the grass, but she was immeasurably moved by the sight of the moors, the mountains and lochs, as though she had been away for years, rather than weeks.

Afraid of betraying the least sign of happiness which Logan might pounce on and destroy, she broke the lengthening silence. 'Your new housekeeper—does she know I'm your wife?'

'She's gone.'

'Gone? But I thought you said she was good?'

'She was—fairly,' he frowned impatiently. Thea was faintly disturbed by his impatient tenseness. 'When she heard about you coming she left. I brought her to Fort William when I came to meet you.'

'But why? I mean, surely you told her I wouldn't be staying?'

A nerve at the corner of his mouth jerked. 'How long you stay had nothing to do with her.' He sighed, a sound of angry frustration. 'I don't think she cared for Drumlarig very much, not after she learnt about you and Jamie broke his leg. I think you were the final straw, or the excuse she'd been looking for. I'm not sure.'

'You don't care?'

'Of course I care!' he snapped, his savagery startling her. 'I don't want you to think I've got you here just to work. You'll have enough to do looking after Jamie. Now you'll be wearing yourself out,' he shot her a grim glance, 'when you appear to be more in need of a rest than any of us.'

There was in her a sudden desire to hurt him, or to try to, as she herself had been hurt. 'I have lost a little weight,' she defended herself with seeming frankness, 'but that was only to be expected. A girl doesn't expect to be married and deserted in practically the same day, but I'm over that now. In fact I'm grateful you brought me to my senses. I'm sure I'll regain any weight I've lost very quickly— probably by the time I leave Drumlarig again.'

'Wait a minute!' With a thick expletive, Logan jammed on the brakes, searching grimly for a place to get off the road. Then, just as she was wondering unsteadily why he wanted to speak to her so urgently, with another tight curse he drove on. 'I'm afraid it will have to wait. My sister-in-law happens to be behind us.'

'Ingrid?'

'The same,' he anticipated Thea's next query curtly. 'Yes, she'll be coming to Drumlarig to visit Jamie.'

'I see.' Uneasily, Thea hesitated. 'Does she know we've split up?'

She felt rather than heard him wince. 'She knows you didn't come back with me from London.' Again there was underlying tension in his voice. 'We have to talk, Thea.'

Forcing an indifferent shrug, which she sensed angered him, she replied, 'Ingrid mightn't dare question you, but she will me. What do I say?'

'Tell her to mind her own damned business.'

'With pleasure,' Thea smiled, yet she could see that the lightness of her answer didn't please him.

At Drumlarig the first thing she did was to run and find Jamie. 'Jamie!' Forgetting, as she had done on other occasions, that he was an eight-year-old boy, she flung her arms around him. To her dismay he clung to her feverishly and burst into tears.

'Oh, Thea,' he cried, 'why did you leave us?'

Having forgotten to ask Logan about that, she didn't know what sort of explanation to give. How did you explain a broken marriage to a small boy? Hadn't he already had one to cope with? Mightn't one more be too much?

Before she could think of a suitable reply, if there was one, Ingrid spoke from behind them. 'What a charmingly touching scene! Lovers' quarrel over, I suppose? All's well that ends well—happily ever after and all that!'

Cringing before such pointed sarcasm, Thea said weakly, 'Every marriage has its ups and downs.'

'After only two days?'

'I—I had business to see to in London.'

'Was that all?'

'Was it, Thea?' Thea became aware of Jamie anxiously repeating Ingrid's question. He was staring at her closely, his small face pale and weary. And she was aware of Logan standing in the doorway, his face taut and expressionless, as usual, but curiously she knew he was waiting as tensely as the others for her answer. A quick anger shook her because Logan was so obviously fearful that she might begin discussing their personal differences in front of the others. His opinion of her must be low.

'Of course,' she answered Jamie swiftly, dragging her eyes away from her husband.

'Then you won't go away again?'

'Oh, Jamie,' she laughed awkwardly, 'I've only just got back!'

This appeared to satisfy him, diverting his attention. Logan helped as he moved quickly to his side and began telling him of friends who had asked about him in Fort William. He had some parcels, too, which Jamie immediately pounced on and began opening. It was almost as if Logan had anticipated such a crisis and prepared for it, Thea thought bitterly.

Throwing off the fur-lined anorak she wore over her jeans, she announced that she would go and make them all a cup of tea. As Jamie glanced up apprehensively, she wondered unhappily how long it would take to restore the trust to his eyes. How much longer, she wondered, even more unhappily, would it take to find some painless way of convincing him that her place wasn't here?

Logan, as she left them, made no attempt to stop her. It seemed he, too, was glad of the respite. Until they decided what to tell Jamie. This must have been what he had wanted to stop about on the road.

Martha exclaimed when she entered the kitchen. 'Ha, I knew you'd be back!'

Trying to keep her voice steady, as the sight of the

kitchen, and Martha, all the dear, familiar things began hitting her painfully, Thea replied sharply, 'I'm not staying for ever. I suppose you know that too?'

'I know the answer, yes.' Old Martha cast a suave glance at the emotion Thea failed to disguise. 'Which is more than you do, my girl, but I'll leave you to find out for yourself.'

By the time Jamie was safely in bed, Thea was so exhausted she would liked to have gone to bed herself. Feeling battered by the events of the day, it was no consolation to know it wasn't yet over. Logan wanted to speak to her, he had told her again after dinner, and she knew if she put him off much longer he was quite capable of coming to her room to seek her out.

He had given her the room next to Jamie's. After showing her to it he had hesitated, murmuring something about it being a temporary arrangement until after they talked. The numbness inside her, making her indifferent, had saved her the bother of assuring him that she would be quite content to stay here alone—until she went away again.

Quickly she rinsed her face and applied a light make-up which she hoped might effectively disguise the thin hollows in her cheeks. Staring in the mirror she saw, almost with surprise, that she still looked beautiful. If anything, the weeks of suffering appeared to have accentuated her good points and fined down the voluptuous lines of her slender young figure. With a careless shrug she turned away.

Going downstairs, she knocked on the library door and entered, not surprised to find Logan in his usual stance beside the fire. His shoulders were bowed, she noticed, and when he turned his face was pale. Quickly he came to draw her forward, pushing her gently down in a chair beside the fire, where she would be warm and comfortable.

His eyes, dwelling on her intently, saw her weariness. 'I don't want you killing yourself,' he asserted tersely. 'I have someone coming to help in the morning.'

His concern might have moved her, but it didn't. 'I'm young and healthy, Logan.' She spoke for the first time.

'You're looking too frail.' His eyes stayed on her even when she moved uneasily. 'Thea, I have to speak to you and I don't know where to begin.' He took a deep breath. 'I don't want to ruin everything by expressing myself badly.'

Steadily she looked at him, grateful that she was able to do this without a quiver. 'You want to speak to me about a divorce. Couldn't it have waited until the morning?'

'Divorce?'

Thea's eyes widened. If she hadn't known better she could have sworn he was completely stunned. 'It's the logical thing to do, isn't it?' she cried. 'Our marriage was a mistake, so there's nothing else for it. You brought me here today because of Jamie, but you don't have to stress that it was only because of him. I already realised . . .'

Hoarsely, Logan interrupted, at last seeming to find his voice, 'It wasn't altogether because of Jamie. Maybe he brought things to a head. Brought me to my senses, would be a better way of putting it.'

In turn, Thea cut in, 'You aren't trying to make me believe you aren't always in control of your senses, Logan, as well as everything else!'

Tautly, he held her dry gaze. 'I deserved that, I guess.'

Her thin shoulders lifted, giving the impression that she wasn't interested enough to argue. 'We don't have to examine every small facet of our individual personalities, Logan.'

'Stop it, Thea!' Swiftly, angrily, he was pulling her to her feet. 'I don't want you talking like this. Or about a divorce, either.'

'It's a free country, and you started it.'

His hands on her arms tightened, his eyes a blaze of

sudden fury. 'All right!' Then, just as quickly as it had risen, his anger left him and he groaned, 'Oh, Thea! I'll admit you're entitled to your pound of flesh, after what I did. I'll admit, after I discovered about your money, my reactions could justifiably be described as outrageous. I can only plead that it was a culmination of many things. My first marriage was no good, you see. I've told you before I was as much to blame as Kay, but while I've always tried to be honest, Kay didn't recognise the meaning of the word. To find you weren't above deceiving me either was like putting a match to a keg of dynamite. I couldn't think straight. I expect it was my pride that wouldn't allow me to, not until I came back here.'

'It took you some time,' she taunted.

He winced at her tone but continued. 'I was mixed up. I didn't sleep, which didn't improve my ability to think. It wasn't until last week, when my aunt died, that it suddenly struck me how short life is. Suddenly I realised I was throwing away the things that really mattered. In London, the day after we were married, I had people to see about some foreign investments I had. When I sold everything I had in that line, in order to buy Drumlarig, they hadn't been worth putting on the market. But mining abroad can be unpredictable. Practically overnight, it seemed, I'd become a wealthy man.'

With a humility Thea could scarcely believe in him, he paused. 'Already I'd discovered how much I loved you —then this. These were the two things I could hardly wait to tell you. I had it all planned. Then, when that man you knew stopped you in the theatre, it was like a slap in the face. I know I shouldn't have acted as I did afterwards, and I had no right to speak to you as I did, either, but you've got to understand that I was half mad with rage and jealousy.'

As he finished, Thea went on looking at him, wondering curiously why none of this had any effect on her. A week or two ago she would have been delirious with joy, but now she didn't feel a thing. 'I'm sorry, Logan,' she whispered.

'Sorry?' Holding her eyes, his own were slightly bewildered. 'Why are you sorry, Thea?'

'Well, it's over, isn't it?'

'Over?' His voice rasped hoarsely, his eyes darkening with passion. 'You can't believe what you're saying Thea. I love you; you told me you loved me. I know I've hurt you desperately, and I'm sorry. If it takes the rest of my life, I swear I'll prove how much.'

'No, Logan.'

'Yes!' Suddenly, his voice roughening, he pulled her into his arms. He didn't kiss her, but he did crush her close, so she could feel his hard muscles pressing into her. Bending his cheek against hers, he pleaded thickly, 'Say you forgive me, my darling. I don't care about your money, you can do what you like with it, and that isn't because I've enough of my own. All I want is your love, and your permission to love you.'

She could feel his lean body shaking. Like her, he had lost weight, but there was still a lot of him. It astonished her to feel him trembling heavily. Even more than she had once done, when he held her.

While he waited for her to speak his arms tightened around her. His mouth stayed taut against her cheek, obviously taking all the control he had in making no attempt to contact hers. It was as if he was leaving this last bit of initiative to her. She had only to turn her lips an inch or so to have them taken by his. When she remembered their wedding night she could have cried. It was all senseless, such sheer waste, but she couldn't pretend what she could no longer feel.

Only for a second did something stir deep inside her, but it was so fleeting as to be easily mistaken for the effort it took to find her voice. 'Let me go, Logan, please. I'm sorry, but I don't love you any more. It's no use pretending that I do.'

His whole body stiffened, as though she had struck him a blow. Sharply he lifted his head to stare down into the cool depth of her grey eyes. His mouth was white as he exclaimed harshly, 'You can't have changed that much so quickly?'

'I have,' she assured him dully.

'No!' his indrawn breath rasped, 'I won't believe it. I felt your love for me. It wasn't an act on our wedding night, Thea. No one could have surrendered as completely as you did without love.' A rough redness came to his cheeks as his voice thickened. 'You were beautiful, my darling. I've wanted you, longed for you, every night since. It's been hell without you.'

Mutely she pushed out of his arms, again shaking her head. Numbly she replied, 'You must have killed what love I felt for you. You have to understand that, Logan. I don't feel anything for you now.'

'Shall I kiss you and find out?' Doubt made his eyes glitter with a stubborn determination. 'I don't think you know what you're talking about.'

If he was throwing out a challenge she couldn't be a coward. Perhaps he had to discover for himself how he was only wasting his time. 'If you like,' she agreed, lifting her mouth like a sacrifice.

She was surprised at how very gentle his lips were, but not surprised that all the instant rapture that had been there before was gone. His hands were on her back, his fingers like steel, almost breaking her. She nearly cried out from pain until she realised it was an unconscious part of the restraint he was imposing on himself, which prevented him from gathering her into a far more passionate embrace.

When he let her go his eyes were dark. He stood staring at her, a muscle at the side of his strongly curved mouth jerking spasmodically, his face grey.

Unevenly she said, 'All I want from you is my freedom.'

'So you can go back to—was it Jerry?'

Strangely his half-hearted sneer hurt her more than any-thing else had done. It also made her uneasy to think she was in any way vulnerable, as far as Logan was concerned. 'No, I won't be going back to Jerry. I just want to be free to lead my own life.' She took a deep breath. 'I'd better tell you, Logan, that I'm arranging to go to university after the summer. Until then I've taken a job on the south coast. I had to let them know I was coming here, but I can still go later.'

He stepped away from her to pour himself a drink. 'I see,' he tossed it off in one go. 'If I took my time you didn't waste any.'

'I rang you, Logan. You know I did. I tried...' Her voice trailed off, as he downed another drink.

He nodded but made no attempt to touch her again. 'I know,' he said harshly. 'More fool me.'

'I'm sorry too, Logan. I realise it was partly my fault, I'm not trying to shove all the blame on to you. I'm really sorry it had to turn out this way. I'll stay for a little while with Jamie, of course.'

'I won't pester you.' His face was stiff, but he appeared to accept her ultimatum. 'I seem to have a genius for making a botch of my life. Two women who hate me! Maybe,' his broad shoulders shrugged, 'it might be a case of third time lucky?'

Thea, for all her continuing indifference, found that Logan's last words haunted her during the next days. As far as the house went, it disturbed her how easily she slipped back into her old routine, but not unduly. Every-thing was so dearly familiar and unchanged—Martha's sharpness, Duncan's dry remarks, even Jamie's chatter. Only Logan was different. She could see he was working too hard. His mines might be making money—certainly all evidence of an unnatural economy at Drumlarig was gone, but it was clear that he wasn't allowing his new affluence to influence the amount of work he did.

One morning, when she dared to mention it, he explained, 'Drumlarig was beginning to pay its way, and I want to continue proving it can do so, without any great injection of capital from a source which has nothing to do with it. I might spend more on the house, one day, if I can find a woman who wants me, but apart from this, for the present anyway, the money from the mines will be reinvested. Put aside, if you like, for a rainy day.'

As her eyes went ironically to the streaming windows, he shrugged. 'Not literally, my dear. Which reminds me, I have work to do and shouldn't be sitting here.' Reaching for his oilskins, he glanced back at her as he went out. 'If Irene calls would you mind telling her that I'll look in and see her this evening. I want to discuss Jamie's new treatment with her.' He paused. 'She seems very good with him, wouldn't you say?'

In all honesty, Thea couldn't deny it. The doctor's daughter was a trained physiotherapist and Jamie looked forward to her visits, the help she gave him. The girl was good with him. It wouldn't be exaggeration to say that a warm camaraderie was developing between them. A twinge of something surprisingly like jealousy caught at Thea's heart, making her flinch, as if from pain. When she went back to London Jamie would need someone. So would Logan, whispered a small voice that she tried to ignore.

When Mrs Murray arrived unexpectedly, Thea felt almost ridiculously glad to see her. Logan had been so unapproachable lately, she hadn't dared ask him what his mother knew of the present situation. When she did find sufficient courage to do so, he merely said curtly that his mother was aware they were having—difficulties.

Thea flinched from the bitterness in his eyes as he spoke. She had a feeling that he wanted to grab her, to

crush her, to shake her, but felt his hands were tied. True
to his word, he hadn't attempted to come near her again
and she could sense him withdrawing daily. Yet he still
continued helping her with many of the heavier tasks about
the house. It often surprised her that he took such care that
she shouldn't get overtired. But, for all she was often conscious of his bleakly unhappy regard, he never tried to
touch her, and each night his footsteps went past her bedroom door without pausing.

Mrs Murray had been there several days before she
brought up the subject Thea had been dreading. They were
alone in the library before tea, having left Jamie talking
happily with a school friend in the drawing-room.

It was a wild afternoon with darkness already gathering. Unable to settle beside the fire, Thea kept glancing
anxiously through the window.

'Is anything wrong?' Mrs Murray asked gently.

Without thinking, Thea replied, 'I do hope Logan isn't
long. It's a terrible night.'

'Isn't he out with some of the men?' Logan had added
to his outdoor staff lately. Calmly Mrs Murray knitted
two more stitches before giving Thea another quick glance.
'Do you worry about him, dear?'

Swiftly, Thea was about to deny it, but suddenly she
couldn't. She did worry over Logan, in so many ways. It
took a lot of believing, but she did. With a stunned expression on her face, she nodded.

'Then why don't you go and find him and tell him so?'
his mother suggested softly.

Helplessly, Thea stared down at her hands, away from
the wise eyes opposite, which seemed to guess so much
without being told. 'I can't!' she gasped, her own eyes wide
and anguished. 'I—I shouldn't be able to. It's as if I
were frozen. I can't feel any more.'

'But you did, then, didn't you?' Gently Mrs Murray
pressed her point, never taking her eyes from the girl's

distraught face. 'I suggested you were anxious and you immediately recognised anxiety within you. Perhaps if you could think of one more thing? Doors are often held by the flimsiest of locks.'

Like someone in a daze, Thea whispered, 'Logan said, when his aunt—your sister died, it made him realise how very short life is.'

Quietly Mrs Murray waited, too wise to interrupt such a pattern of thought.

Tremulously, feeling torn, Thea considered silently. If Logan didn't return? If he met with an accident out there on the moors, where weather such as this could mean very real danger. If he should be carried away from her, as his aunt had been, from her loved ones, what would she do? What price her pride and her frozen heart then?

With a strangled cry she jumped to her feet, running almost blindly from the room. What a fool she had been, oh, what a fool! She still loved Logan. Wherever he was she must find him and tell him. He might not love her any more, but she had to tell him!

He was out on the moors, by the loch, moving sheep. Again, as she had done on the day she had gone to meet Jamie, Thea splashed through the flooding river. She knew about the bridge, but had no time to go around by it.

It was raining, but she hadn't stopped to find a coat. All she could see was Logan on his great black horse. The wind tore through his hair as he shouted something to the men who were with him, the rain streaming down his cheeks. It was cold, very cold, but she was only aware of the ice around her heart melting.

'Logan!' she screamed wildly.

Whether it was instinct, or the wind carrying her voice, she didn't know, but suddenly the black horse wheeled and he was beside her. He scooped her up as though she was as light as a feather, holding her closely in front of him, shielding her shaking body with his big one from the worst of the elements.

'Thea?' as she sobbed painfully against him, his voice came deeply urgent, striving to quieten her. 'What's wrong? You're wet through! Tell me!'

'Nothing, Logan. Oh, everything!' Clutching at him with feverish hands, she found herself unable to speak. What if he didn't want her? The confusion that swept her seemed worse than the wind and the rain, but she forced herself to go on. 'I had to come! I discovered that I love you again.'

For a moment he sat as though he had been turned to stone, then, with a harsh gasp, his arms tightened. His hand drove fiercely through her hair, pulling her urgently against him as he bent violently over her. Even before he spoke she could feel his heart pounding right through her.

'Thank God,' he said grimly. 'Thea, girl, you don't know what I've been through, how much I've longed to hear you say that. I couldn't bear to think that I'd lost you, but nothing I tried seemed to have any effect. I was slowly dying, feeling desperate, until I saw you running through the water to me. Only then did I dare wonder if I had my old reckless Thea back.'

She was powerless in the strength of his hold, but she wanted nothing else. 'It must have been shock, Logan.'

His voice was still grim. 'I knew what it was. What I didn't know was how much longer I could stand it. You don't know what I suffered, my darling, having to walk past your bedroom door each night.'

'I love you,' she whispered. 'Feel my heart racing if you don't believe me. Please never let me go again.'

'Never!' he promised thickly, then his head blotted out the dark moorland, the men and sheep disappearing in the distance, as his lips pressed savagely on hers, his kisses no less wild than the night.

Later, in the warmth of the stables, he took her in his arms again and it was some time before he let her go. The urgency of his need got through to her, not only in what he said but from the pressure of his hands and mouth. As he pressed her mouth open, desire stirred within her, throbbing madly through her body, and a tremulous surge of love sent her arms passionately around his neck. Never again would she think of leaving him, never again would she let him believe he could let her go.

'You need a hot bath,' he said, his hands on her damp shirt, 'and so do I.' As they left the stable, he bent to whisper something in her ear that made her cheeks colour to a rosy glow.

Her cheeks were still pink as they walked into the kitchen. One look at their faces and both Mrs Murray and Martha smiled.

Pausing, with Logan's arm still around her, Thea glanced up at him apprehensively. There was still something to be cleared up. She had almost forgotten about it, but nothing must be allowed to get in the way of their future happiness. Better to confess now than risk Logan's anger later. Her smile fading, she began quite incoherently, 'I have to confess I've been here before.'

The small, rather puzzled silence that greeted her stilted announcement was broken sharply by Martha.

'You were born here, weren't you? As soon as I saw you I knew who you were—which was more than anybody else seemed to do.'

'You knew?' Thea felt dazed, moving towards her.

'As soon as you walked through that door,' Martha indicated the one leading to the hall. 'But I couldn't say anything until you did.' She turned to a startled Mrs Murray. 'Don't you remember the girl who came here over twenty years ago, after her husband had been killed on their honeymoon, when they ran away together? This is the baby she had—the child it almost broke your heart to

...en her mother took her with her when she

...y whispered, 'Can this be true?'

...odded numbly to Mrs Murray's astonished query, Logan's mother took her in her arms and kissed her gently. 'What Martha says is quite right,' she smiled. 'I would have liked you for my own daughter. I'm afraid I even begged to be allowed to adopt you. Now I do believe in miracles!'

After listening to Thea's halting explanations, she hugged her warmly again before letting her go. Rubbing happy tears from her eyes, she went to the cupboard, declaring that the occasion called for nothing less than champagne but they might have to make do with sherry.

Throughout, Logan had been silent. Half afraid, Thea dared at last to turn and look at him. Mrs Murray had been so carried away she had obviously forgotten about him. To Thea's surprise and relief she found he was smiling, as though content and not over troubled to have found the answer to her mysterious appearance in November.

'Do you believe me?' she faltered anxiously.

'Come here, minx,' he teased softly, holding out his arms, taking no notice of the other occupants of the kitchen. 'I'll believe you, if you can convince me that you'll never run away again.'

And she did!

The Mills & Boon Rose is the Rose of Romance

Every month there are ten new titles to choose from — ten new stories about people falling in love, people you want to read about, people in exciting, far-away places. Choose Mills & Boon. It's your way of relaxing:

November's titles are:

IMAGES OF LOVE *by Anne Mather*
Tobie couldn't resist seeing Robert Lang again, to exact her revenge — but she didn't know what had happened to Robert since they had last met ...

BRAND OF POSSESSION *by Carole Mortimer*
Jake Weston's lack of trust in her ought to have killed all the love Stacy felt for him — but it didn't.

DIFFICULT DECISION *by Janet Dailey*
Deborah knew that her job as secretary to the forceful Zane Wilding would be difficult — but the real challenge was to her emotions ...

HANNAH *by Betty Neels*
Nurse Hannah Lang was happy to accompany the van Eysinks back to Holland, but the unbending Doctor Valentijn van Bertes was not quite so enthusiastic about it.

A SECRET AFFAIR *by Lilian Peake*
As a confidential secretary, Alicia was well aware how essential it was to keep secret about her boss's new project. So why didn't he trust her?

THE WILD MAN *by Margaret Rome*
Rebel soon realised how Luiz Manchete had earned his name — the wild man — when she found herself alone with him in the heart of his jungle kingdom ...

STRANGER IN THE NIGHT *by Charlotte Lamb*
When Clare met Macey Janson, she began to lose some of her fear of men. So why did Luke Murry have to turn up again, making Macey suspect the worst of her?

RACE AGAINST LOVE *by Sally Wentworth*
Toni disliked Adam Yorke intensely, and her friend Carinna was more than welcome to him! But did Toni *really* mean that?

DECEPTION *by Margaret Pargeter*
Sick to death of being run after for her money, Thea ran away herself — but she only found a new set of problems ...

FROZEN HEART *by Daphne Clair*
Joining an expedition to the Antarctic, Kerin was taken aback to discover that the arrogant Dain Ransome was to be its leader ...

Mills & Boon Classics

The very best of Mills & Boon
romances, brought back for those of you
who missed reading them when they
were first published.
In
November
we bring back the following four
great romantic titles.

SAVAGE LAND
by Janet Dailey

When Coley left the city for a cattle ranch in Texas she was
prepared to find certain changes in her way of life. But she
was to find that dealing with the brooding Jason Savage was
to bring her greater problems than even she had anticipated ...

DARK MOONLESS NIGHT
by Anne Mather

Seven years ago Caroline had considered Gareth Morgan
unsuitable as a husband for herself. Now they had met again
in the African jungle and Caroline's feelings had changed. But
the disturbing Gareth told her she would be wasting her time
trying to rekindle old fires ...

THE TOWER OF THE CAPTIVE
by Violet Winspear

Don Rafael had a Spanish attitude towards the amount of
freedom women should have, and Vanessa had an Anglo-Saxon
attitude. This was all right — until Vanessa fell in love with
Rafael.

PARISIAN ADVENTURE
by Elizabeth Ashton

It was perhaps because of Renée's resemblance to the famous
model, Antoinette, that she found herself transported suddenly
from London to the salons of Paris. The famous couturier,
Léon Sebastien, needed a replacement for Antoinette and Renée
filled the bill. Rumour also had it that Léon needed a
replacement for Antoinette in more ways than one!

If you have difficulty in obtaining any of these books through
your local paperback retailer, write to:

Mills & Boon Reader Service
P.O. Box 236, Thornton Road, Croydon, Surrey, CR9 3RU.

Masquerade
Historical Romances

Intrigue
excitement
romance

LADY IN THE LION'S DEN
by Elaine Reeve

When the proud Norman lady Adela de Lise was
kidnapped by the Saxon rebel calling himself Leowulf,
Lord of Erinwald, she refused to submit tamely. Then
she discovered that he intended to buy his own safety
by making her his wife . . .

UNWILLING BETROTHAL
by Christine James

Annabelle Sarne was doubly an heiress, but she had no
objection to becoming betrothed to her cousin Gaspard
— after all, she had loved him for years. But the
Revolution forced her to flee from France to England,
and there she encountered a man who had a prior
claim to her hand — and he refused to relinquish it!

Look out for these titles in your local paperback shop from
14th November 1980